LOST POND

BOOKS BY

MARK W. HOLDREN

*

Spirit Wolf

The Raven

Lost Pond

Order through your bookseller
or at www.powellhillpress.com

LOST POND

BY

MARK W. HOLDREN

Powell Hill Press
Fairport, NY
www.powellhillpress.com

iii

ISBN 978-0-9760648-2-4

Library of Congress Control Number 2009923777

Powell Hill Press
8 Packett's Glen
Fairport, NY 14450
www.powellhillpress.com

Lost Pond is a work of fiction. Places, events and situations in this story are purely fictional. Any resemblance to actual persons living or dead is purely coincidental.

Cover design by Richard C. Burandt (www.richardburandt.com)
and Jeremy Sniatecki (www.bullcreekstudios.com)
Locomotive back cover photo by Thomas K. Kraemer
(www.rrtraxstudios.com)
Author photo by Gary Whelpley.

Printed in the United States of America

Dedication

For Kelly and Kara

Acknowledgements

No book is written alone. The author wishes to express his heartfelt thanks and gratitude to Marie-France Etienne, Richard C. Burandt, Jeremy Sniatecki, Julie Stoltz, Lynne Bellucsio, Jennifer Taylor, Thomas K. Kraemer, Wendy Low, Ruth Thaler-Carter and Kat Nagel. Their encouragement and support helped bring *Lost Pond* to life.

Prologue

The Canadian Flyer, pride of the Adirondack Railway and Steamship Company, was running late. Seth Adams raised his pocket watch into the faint glow of a kerosene lantern that was swinging lazily to the rhythm of the rails. It was nearly midnight.

"Shoulda cleared Lost Pond by now," he muttered.

Seth Adams, senior engineer, didn't like being late.

But the Flyer, bound for Montreal, had made an unscheduled stop. Adams stuck his head from the cab. The cold clawed at his face like a churlish cat. Squinting into the swirling snow he could just see the Otter River trestle coming into the flickering light of the rumbling locomotive's head lamp. That put the isolated settlement of Lost Pond still eight miles away.

"It's von Koenig's railroad," shouted fireman Tommy Palermo as he shoveled more coal into the firebox. "If he wants his train stopped, we stop it."

Leaving Utica that afternoon, Adams had been handed a note:

Pick up passenger at Eagle's Nest

The note wasn't signed. No signature was required. Eagle's Nest was the summer estate and hunting preserve of Erik von Koenig, builder and principal owner of the burgeoning Adirondack Railway and Steamship Company. He was also the largest single land owner in the Adirondacks North Country, holding more than half a million acres of timber and watershed lands. The Austrian-born von Koenig had employed more than a dozen master German stonemasons to build his imperial eighty-room mansion. It rose from the summit of Mount Lorraine—named after von Koenig's regally voluptuous wife—as if it had been carved by hand from the windswept peak's twin granite dome. Western elk, imported from Wyoming, roamed the 200,000-acre estate. A ten-foot-high fence kept von Koenig's game in and would-be poachers out. Eagle's Nest Station was marked PRIVATE on the railroad's schedule. It was located at mile marker seventy-five on the nearly 250-mile Utica-Montreal line. Rail passengers couldn't buy a ticket to Eagle's Nest. If you weren't invited, you didn't get off. Adams had thought it highly unusual to be stopping there, let alone picking up a passenger. Eagle's Nest was normally shuttered following the September hunt, its owner and his moneyed guests off to warmer, more hospitable climes. Yet when he'd eased the Flyer to a stop an hour earlier, he'd seen von Koenig himself standing off to the side of the loading platform. Aharon Friedman, von Koenig's treasurer and trusted aide, was also there. And there was a third man, lingering in the shadows. He was armed with a double-barrel shotgun. Adams thought it might have been Louie LaMont, von Koenig's favorite guide and the estate's winter caretaker. Adams had started to climb down to stretch his legs.

"I suggest you remain in the cab. Your passenger will be riding back there," Friedman had said, pointing back to the caboose. Brakeman Frank Hutchins should have been riding there, keeping a sharp eye on the train and firewood in the pot-bellied stove. But Frank had called in sick. As far as Adams knew, Frank Hutchins hadn't been sick a day in his life. Louie

LaMont, if it was indeed him, would be riding alone, Adams had thought. And it would be a cold trip, unless he fired up the stove himself. Adams had done what he was told; he'd ducked back into the cab. But as soon as Friedman had turned, Adams had taken another look. He saw the man with the shotgun climb into the caboose. Then he watched von Koenig hand the man four satchel-sized bags.

Now, crossing the Otter River, Adams was still wondering what Erik von Koenig could possibly be shipping to Canada. What was in those satchels that required an armed guard of LaMont's steely reputation?

Seth Adams settled back into his seat.

The Canadian Flyer thundered north.

But when the pride of the Adirondack Railway and Steamship Company pulled into Montreal's Central Station shortly after 3 a.m., Louie LaMont and the mysterious cargo entrusted to him were long gone.

Chapter One

NEW YORK CITY. OCTOBER 1, 2007

"Good morning, Munson…garage please."

Munson was already closing the elevator's door.

"Yes sir, Mr. Flynn."

Munson's smile was wide and his curiosity, as always, insatiable. His keen eye had already noted that I was dressed in jeans and a light fleece pullover, and that I was carrying a duffle, not my usual briefcase. But he asked nonetheless, "Business or pleasure?"

Business? I thought. Munson didn't know I'd just been fired.

Harrington & Hall, the darling of Wall Street investment banks, was bleeding billions in subprime mortgage losses. Someone had to fall on their sword. And it wouldn't be J.W. Harrington, the firm's founder, chairman and CEO. So he canned hundreds of us in a single day. He'd conveniently forgotten the futures department I headed had nothing to do with the firm's staggering losses. Stephanie, my live-in partner—and J.W. Harrington's youngest daughter—had a memory lapse as well. We were to be married Christmas Eve. But she'd dumped me the day after her father gave me the ax. So I was taking time to readjust, as they say. The cards were falling my way at poker. The game was played in a deliciously smoke-filled room at Michael Shea's, an Irish joint off Liberty Street. I was up more than a grand. And the Red Sox were in town for a three-game stand. Why rush back to work? I hadn't given back the firm's Yankee's tickets. Screw J.W.

1

Harrington.

"I'm driving Upstate," I told Munson, "a family matter."

Munson rubbed at the side of his fist-flattened nose with the back of a meaty left hand. Munson had been a contender, a promising middleweight. Then he was beaten half to death in a Cleveland ring. That was more than twenty years ago. He'd had his shot. He wouldn't get another. Munson had been answering an elevator bell ever since.

"So where'd you say you was going?" he asked. Munson still kept punching.

"Lost Pond," I replied.

His scarred eyelids narrowed. "Lost what? That some kinda place?"

"You can't get there from here," I joked.

Munson flashed me a smile, then a blazing right jab. It was a punch he playfully pulled an inch from my jaw.

"It's in the Adirondacks...in the middle of nowhere," I added, handing him my tickets to the rest of the Yankee-Red Sox series. "I can't use these where I'm going."

"Hey, thanks," Munson said, sliding the tickets into his pocket. "You the man!"

We passed the eleventh...tenth...the ninth floor. Munson threw another punch. "Got family...in this Lost Pond place?"

"My grandfather, Rufus," I replied. "He's been living in some cabin up there for nearly ten years."

Munson looked surprised. "He must be an old-timer."

I was thirty-one, but looked well north of forty.

"Was an old-timer," I replied. "He died a week ago. I'm going up there to settle his affairs."

"I'm sorry," Munson said. I could tell he meant it.

The elevator eased to a stop. I picked up my duffle and stepped into the cold garage.

"Thanks again for the tickets, Mr. Flynn. Hope you can

find…Lost Pond," Munson added with a grin.

"Very funny," I replied. "See you in a couple of days."

■   ■   ■

I'd learned about Pop's death just yesterday. The call had come in the bottom of the fifth. *Christ, not now,* I'd thought. A-Rod had just stepped to the plate. He was casting a cold stare at Boston's Josh Beckett, who was kicking at the mound like a menacing bull. Damon was at first, Jeter at third. The Yankees trailed by two. The *House that Ruth Built* was rockin'. The caller had sounded just slightly drunk. His name was Ingram, but I could call him Doc, he'd said. He told me he was a friend of my grandfather's and that he was calling from Lost Pond. Ingram hadn't given me much information, only that my grandfather was gone. He didn't say how he'd died or why no one had bothered to call me until now. But that shouldn't have surprised me, given my grandfather's raging eccentricity and his love of oddball characters like himself. That's probably why he'd ended up living out the rest of his life in a place like Lost Pond. Ingram had asked about the noise at my end.

"A-Rod just hit one out of the park," I'd shouted.

"Rufus loved his Yankees," Ingram had said.

Yeah, he did, I'd thought. *And I never found the time to have him down for a game. Now he was gone.* I remember feeling like a real shithead.

I still do.

"Your grandfather was insistent that you settle his affairs," Ingram had said. "Called you some kind of financial genius," he'd added.

When I'd asked Ingram about my grandfather's body, about any arrangements, he said that we had more to talk

3

about. Then he hung up.

My grandparents had split a dozen years ago, signing their separation agreement one week shy of their fiftieth wedding anniversary. But their troubles had begun nearly a decade earlier. That's when Pop—I'd called my grandfather Pop since I was two years old—walked away from the advertising agency he'd founded in Rochester some thirty years earlier.

"Too many of my friends are already dead," he'd said. "I have more living to do."

While Pop had been building his business, working sixteen-hour days, much of it spent on the road or entertaining clients two or three nights a week, my grandmother was raising my father and creating a life of her own. When Pop retired, they discovered they no longer had much in common. That's when my grandfather lit out for the territory, as he put it—kayaking in Alaska, rafting the Grand Canyon, and fishing the great rivers of the West. Rumors of one girlfriend, then another, soon followed. Finally my grandmother had simply had enough. She booted him out for good. It was no surprise that Pop had chosen to spend the rest of his days in the Adirondacks. He'd tramped the North Country of New York state most of his life. And I was lucky enough to have tagged along with him until I was fifteen. Then my mother remarried. We moved to Denver. I never saw Pop again. That was my fault, not his. He'd had invited me up to his cabin a dozen times or more.

"You need to learn what I've learned; you need to awaken to your life's true purpose," he kept telling me.

But I wasn't listening. I was too busy making money on Wall Street and romancing my boss's daughter. Oh, I called Pop on his birthday and at Christmas. But I owed my grandfather a hell of a lot more. He was the father I never had, my parents having divorced when I was six. As far as I knew,

Pop had been living alone. One of his girlfriends did give it a try. Lynne Brewster didn't last long.

"Couldn't take the winters," Pop had told me shortly after he'd arrived in Lost Pond. "I think she's living with some Navajo shaman in Taos," he'd laughed.

I was missing him more than I could ever have imagined.

Chapter Two

It was just past eight. The Hudson River glistened in the soft morning light. I was crossing the George Washington Bridge into New Jersey. I'd thought about flying, but Lost Pond was hours from airports in Albany or Syracuse. So taking my vintage Corvette seemed the only intelligent option. I hadn't driven it much since moving to Manhattan. Who would drive a '65 Sting Ray in New York City? I'd purchased it from its original owner four years ago in LA. It was rally red and just nudging thirty-thousand miles. The original sticker price was just under five grand. It was worth ten times that now. Pop and I had fished the Hudson a couple of times for brown trout, hiking into the gorge above North River. There the Hudson ran cold and clear. But the river running beneath the GW was now a near-toxic mix of sewage and chemical waste. Its journey past Fort Edward, Troy, Albany, Kingston and Poughkeepsie had taken a terrible toll. I was glad to be traveling upstream. Pop had taught me to fly fish in the shadow of Whiteface Mountain, drifting nymphs in the rushing pocket water of the Ausable River. We'd fished the quieter water of the nearby Saranac, too. I was wishing now that I'd brought along my fly rod. The fly rod Pop had sent me as a college graduation gift. The fly rod I'd never used.

Mapquest estimated my trip from the city to a place called Loon Landing at 310.42 miles or about five and a half hours. That's where the road stopped and so did Mapquest's directions. From there I'd have to ride by boat to Lost Pond.

I flipped on my radar detector and let the Corvette loose. Twenty minutes later, I'd cleared Jersey and was heading northwesterly across New York state toward Albany. The ubiquitous sprawl of shopping malls and cookie-cutter bedroom communities gradually was giving way to rolling hillsides splashed in brilliant autumn colors. The city was definitely behind me. Pop's death was puzzling me. Sure, he'd just turned eighty-three. I'd called to wish him a happy birthday. That was in early July. He'd grumbled about too many summer people, but admitted that was a good thing. "We need their money," he'd said. He was feeling fine, he'd told me. For someone who probably drank too much and smoked too many cigars, he'd always been in remarkable health. I hoped that I'd inherited his genes. He'd told me he was working on a little project. He might need my help. He didn't elaborate, only that what he'd discovered would change history. I'd written off his last remark to his usual bravado. But what did this Doc Ingram mean, *more to talk about?* What did he know that he wasn't telling me? Why did a week elapse between my grandfather's death and Ingram calling me? And what had been done with the body?

The five hundred bucks I'd paid for the radar detector was already paying dividends. New York State's Thruway may be the most over patrolled roadway in America. I hadn't been in the Empire State an hour and already I'd hit the brakes for two deviously concealed speed traps. Why weren't the state's troopers chasing bad guys instead of harassing tax-paying citizens like me who just liked to drive fast? Thanks to my wise investment and a keen eye, I managed to exit the Thruway at Utica unscathed. Stopping at an E-Z Mart on Route 12, I gassed up, hit the men's room and grabbed a cup of coffee. The air was clean and crisp. The hoary remnants of the night's killing frost were still clung to the potted marigolds that graced the store's doorway. Under way again, I hung a right onto NY Route 28 at Alder Creek. A state marker soon

7

welcomed me to the Adirondack Park. The Corvette hugged the twisting, two-lane highway like a long-lost lover. Together we wound our way into the largest protected wilderness area east of the Mississippi. Towering pines embraced both sides of the road, their arrow-like spires rising majestically into a cobalt autumn sky.

"The mountains are calling, and we must go," Pop would say, his way of telling me it was time for us to head for the Adirondacks. When he wasn't teaching me to fish, we were climbing Mount Marcy, Algonquin, Haystack and a dozen others. But our favorite climb was more a mound than a mountain. It's called Mount Frederica and overlooks Lake Lila in almost the geographic center of the Adirondack Park. We'd kayak to the west end of the lake and then make the mile-and-a-half climb to the mostly sun-drenched summit. There we'd kick back on the warm slabs of granite and watch the wind swirl across the lake below. Pop would light a cigar, much to the dismay of anyone sharing the view with us.

"It doesn't get any better than this, Ryan," he'd tell me. "Another day in paradise."

■　　■　　■

I was lucky to spot the sign. It was hand-painted on a slab of split pine.

Loon Landing
18 Miles

It was hanging from a power pole in the mountain hamlet of Little Moose, about an hour northwest of Utica. Little Moose was aptly named. There was a Big M grocery store, a gas station and a tavern, Molly and Lefty's, which occupied a log-cabin style building that also served as a post office. That was it. I followed the yellow arrow on the sign and turned left, leaving Route 28 behind me. The frost-heaved pavement was dappled with leaves, crimson reds and pale yellows that rained down from the maples and yellow birches that lined both sides of road. I passed an assortment of modest camps, some in serious disrepair. But as the road climbed toward the ridgeline, the woods closed in around me.

I drove on.

■　　■　　■

The next sign caught me by surprise.

CAUTION!
Pavement Ends Ahead

Shit.

I wasn't halfway to Loon Landing. Driving the Corvette was now a very dumb idea. The road took a sharp right-hand turn. I dropped off the asphalt onto a roadbed of loose stones, some the size of golf balls. Downshifting to second, then to first gear didn't help. The road was fighting our intrusion, pummeling the Vette's side panels and undercarriage with stones.

Shit!

Slowing to a crawl, maintaining just enough rpms to keep the motor from stalling, I began weaving my way through a minefield of gaping potholes and jagged rocks. I'd gone about a mile and was climbing a steep rise in the road when a logging truck thundered over the other side. It was headed straight for me. There wasn't going to be room enough for the two of us. I yanked on the steering wheel and headed for a shallow ditch. The rocks clawed at the undercarriage and ripped at the mufflers and tailpipes. I slammed on the brakes.

The logger roared by in a hailstorm of stones as a cloud of soup-thick yellowish dust settled over me.

"Bastard," I shouted, turning on the wipers.

The logger had left his calling card; there was a deep chip in the windshield just under the rearview mirror. It was the size of a half dollar.

"You asshole," I said. I was speaking of myself, of course, for driving the Corvette instead of renting an SUV or a pickup.

I began easing my way from the ditch, but another logger was already taking a bead on me.

And I was a sitting duck.

He stormed past me. I could see his bobbing head up in the cab. He was laughing. I wondered if I was the object of some twisted North Country welcome, reserved for city slickers in fancy cars. The choking dust was overwhelming the Corvette's ventilation system. It was seeping through the vents and descending over the dash and seats like my mother's turkey gravy. I stayed put. Three or four minutes passed. Then a soft breeze began blowing the dust cloud off into the woods. I climbed from the car to check the damage. The driver's side window was still intact, but the door was cracked in several places. There were three rippling cracks in the hood, and the roof looked like someone had worked it over with a rake.

"Asshole!"

There was a faint trail leading off into the woods. I thought I could use a walk. After making my way through a thicket of yellow birch trees I discovered a clearing about a quarter acre in size. There were the remnants of an old campfire, and a wide view across the valley to the east. A deer bolted from its resting place beneath a white pine. Its dusky white horns flashed in the mid-day sun. And then it was gone, vanishing into the woods. Taking a whiz, I watched a turkey

10

vulture cruising on the thermals overhead. It was no doubt waiting to pick at my bones when the loggers were through stoning me to death. I headed back for the car before it could get a piece of me.

The road didn't get any better, but I didn't have to play chicken with any more playful loggers. A couple of canoe-packing SUVs and a battered pickup with an aluminum boat dangling over its tailgate rumbled past me, but there was enough road for all of us. Twenty minutes later, the gravel road intersected with pavement, of sorts. There was a bullet-ravaged metal sign. It was dangling by a single nail from a rotting T-shaped pine post:

LAKE MOHAWK
Loon Landing .5 Miles

An arrow appeared to be pointing right. I headed that way.

Chapter Three

The road might have been paved, but not lately. One too many North Country winters had heaved its scarred surface into a maze of melon-shaped humps and gaping cracks. Loon Landing's best days had clearly passed. Its outskirts were mostly abandoned ramshackle wood-frame structures, their exterior walls peeling paint like sun-ravaged skin. The road dissolved into an oil and stone parking lot the size of a football field. It was pretty much empty but for three pickup trucks, a jeep, and perhaps half a dozen empty boat trailers. I checked my watch. It was just after one. Surprisingly I'd bested Mapquest's ETA by half an hour. Shutting off the motor, I climbed from the car to inspect the damage. My vintage Corvette was a goddamned mess. I was looking at thousands in fiberglass work, a new windshield, a complete new paint job.

What a friggin' mistake!

I slammed the door and looked around. There was a boat livery of sorts, Roy's Marina. It was a low log building built over a crumbling cement pier that looked like it might succumb to the lake at any minute. There was a bar and restaurant, too. Things were looking up. The Tumble Inn occupied a grassy hillside not far from the marina. There wasn't a soul in sight. Whitecaps were coursing over the lake, now the color of cold gray steel under a suddenly sullen sky. Near the boat launch the State of New York Department of Environmental Conservation had erected an information kiosk. It was crafted of pine logs. I walked over to take a look. There was a map of the lake, which appeared to lay pretty much east and west. But for the settlement of Lost Pond, some ten miles away—at the eastern tip of the Lake Mohawk—and where I stood at Loon Landing, the shoreline of the lake was protected wilderness. The map indicated there were forty campsites, accessible by boat only. There was a stern message:

Carry it in. Carry it out.
Leave nothing behind but footprints.

There was a smaller kiosk nearby, a self-regulating check-in system for campers. Its walls were posted with ominous warnings—bears, beaver fever, giardiasis, and high winds were noted in bold black type. I walked to the shore. The sand was the color of dark tea, the beach sprinkled with small, ebony stones. I picked one up. It was smooth as a marble, polished by centuries of wind and water. A pair of mergansers paddled furiously past the pier. Then, relenting to the waves, they splashed off the roiling water and flew off down the lake. Ingram had asked me to call him when I arrived at the Landing. He'd send a boat to pick me up. I tried my cell. No signal. So I headed for the bar at the Tumble Inn.

A red neon sign—OPEN—was hanging in one corner of a wide picture window facing the water, a welcome beacon no doubt for weary campers calling it quits on the lake. Unlike most of Loon Landing's structures, the Tumble Inn appeared to be in good repair. Its roof was made of green corrugated metal. The two-story frame building was freshly painted, the siding white, the shutters forest green. Marigolds and petunias were still flourishing in a dozen birch bark flower boxes. The log-trimmed wood deck overlooking the lake was fitted with round plastic tables, their umbrellas heralding the brand names of several makers of beer and booze.

I walked through the front door and into the bar. The

dining room—with perhaps a dozen round wood tables dressed in red and white checker tablecloths—was off to the right. A doorway to my left opened to a game room complete with a large pool table, dart boards and a pinball machine. The barroom was small, with no more than 10 stools. It was paneled in knotty pine lathered in enough polyurethane that its walls glistened like glass. The back bar was anchored by a century-old steel cash register. Just above it hung the stuffed head of a white-tail deer. A Mexican sombrero was dangling from one of its ten horns. The beer cooler was shaped like a beer bottle and was painted appropriately brown. It was about six feet high with a long glass door, affording a good view of the brands available. A sign hanging near the cash register suggested would be thieves or troublemakers take their business elsewhere:

Security by Smith & Wesson

There was a single lighted beer sign. Like the cash register and bottle cooler, it was an antique. Most of the gold leaf coating on its metal frame had long ago peeled away. There was a plastic insert—a painted illustration of a leaping brook trout in a rushing mountain stream. The sign was cracked in two places. Cigarette and cigar smoke had tainted the plastic mustard yellow. The owners probably kept it up for Pop. Genesee Beer. He drank nothing but. He called his Genny Red Eyes, referring to a once-prominent red logo on Genesee Beer's mostly white can.

A woman burst from the kitchen into the bar.

"Can I help you?"

She was in her early sixties, I guessed. Her hair was jet black, held back in a pony tail. She was wearing a red T-shirt and white Bermuda shorts, which accented her tanned, muscular legs. She was clearly bra-less, her ample breasts heaving with her long stride.

"Do you have a phone? I can't raise a bar on my cell."

"You can thank the tree huggers for that," she snapped. "We've been trying to get a tower built for years...disguised as a pine tree for Christ's sake! But the greenies still won't go for it. I'm all for the environment, but give me a friggin' break."

I detected the remnants of a Brooklyn accent.

She took a closer look at me with her misty brown eyes.

"You must be Rufus' grandson," she said matter-of-factly. "Doc said to keep an eye out for you."

She took a bottle of Labatt's from the cooler, twisted off the cap and flipped it expertly with her thumb into a wastebasket some ten feet away.

"Nice shot," I offered.

"Never miss," she replied. "Join me?" She took a long, deep swig from the bottle.

I pointed at the old sign. "How 'bout a Red Eye?"

She laughed. "You knew the Roof, that's for sure. I'm sorry about your grandfather," she added. "He was one of my all-time favorites."

"Thanks," I replied. "Where's the phone? This Doc Ingram asked me to call him when I got in. Said he'd send a boat to take me out to Lost Pond."

"You can ride out with Arlo Stoner," she said, sliding my bottle of Genny and a tulip-shaped glass down the bar.

"Rufus always drank his beer from a glass, said it tasted better that way," she said, again flipping the cap into the wastebasket.

"He was right," I replied, filling the glass, topping it off with a nice head, then emptying half of it in three swallows.

"Arlo should be along any minute," she said. "*La Mouche Noire* is out of snails."

"La Mouche what?"

"It's French for The Black Fly. It's a restaurant, the only restaurant...out there," she added, pointing a spear-like pink fingernail toward the lake. "Hakeem—he's Arlo's partner—is one hell of a chef, trained in Paris and New York."

"You're telling me there's a French restaurant out there, in the middle of nowhere?" I asked.

"Pretty eclectic crowd...out there," she replied.

I polished off my beer. The first one always goes fast. Without asking she got me another. She didn't forget herself.

"You sound a little...New York," I said. "Brooklyn?"

"Flatbush, born and raised." She extended her hand. "Cheyenne...Cheyenne Levine."

Her hand was soft and warm, but she had the grip of a lumberjack.

"Ryan Flynn," I said.

"Rufus said you lived in the city."

I nodded. No sense in getting into the messy details. "So this Arlo and Hakeem run a French restaurant called...*La Mouche Noire*?" I asked.

"No, Arlo's a guide. It's Hakeem's restaurant."

"I thought you said they were partners?" I asked.

"That's what I said," she replied.

"Oh." I replied, thinking *a gay mountain guide...well, why not?*

"So how does a girl from Flatbush end up in Loon Landing?" I asked.

Cheyenne Levine plucked a thin cigar from a metal box on the back bar. She bit off the tip and spit it into the wastebasket. Striking a wood match on the cash register, she lit up and enjoyed a long, contemplative puff.

"Bernie, my husband, and I started coming up here in the early seventies, snowmobiling...always stayed here at the hotel. When Fritz...Fritz Wheeler decided to sell and move to Arizona, we thought, what the hell. That was in 1991."

She took another swig of beer followed by a long drag on the cigar.

"We fixed the place up, new plumbing, that sort of thing, added the game room and rebuilt the deck. Bernie was a carpenter, so he did most of the work himself. I do miss him."

"Miss him?" I asked, polishing off my Red Eye.

"Lost Bernie three years ago," she replied. "He went through the ice on his snowmobile," she added, with a nod toward the lake. "Never found his body, what with the currents and all. He's still...out there, somewhere." She tipped her beer bottle toward the window. "Love you, Bernie." She turned quickly away and wiped a tear from her cheek.

The door swung open.

"I've been here long enough, where's my drink?"

He was a sinewy man with a smartly trimmed red beard. He slammed the door behind him and loped toward the bar like a wolf. Cheyenne Levine already had a bottle of Knob Creek bourbon in one hand and a short glass in the other.

"Arlo Stoner, you son of a bitch," she bellowed. "Say hello to Ryan Flynn. Arlo here's the best damn guide in the Adirondacks."

Stoner clamped down on my hand like a vice. His skin felt like the shag bark on a hickory tree. He was six feet, maybe a bit more, and probably in his late thirties. He was wearing green wool pants with black leather suspenders and a red flannel shirt. His wide-brimmed brown felt hat—festooned with a colorful assortment of fishing flies—was tipped down over his forehead.

This guy is right out of central casting, I thought.

"Doc said I might catch you," Stoner said. He downed Cheyenne's generous shot of bourbon. She poured him another. "That your Vette out there...sixty-five, isn't it?" he asked.

Arlo Stoner had an eye for cars.

"Doc didn't warn me about the road," I replied. "A couple of loggers got their jollies off with me."

Stoner tipped his glass toward my nose. "Welcome to the North Country." He swallowed his bourbon and slammed the glass down on the bar.

"I believe I'll have another, for the road...so to speak."

Cheyenne obliged, and then poured a shot for herself and for me. "Here's to Rufus. He was one hell of a son of a bitch."

"I'll drink to that," Stoner added.

We threw down the shots.

"Best be heading back," Stoner said. "Don't want to get caught in that storm that's rollin' in."

I reached for my wallet.

"Forget it. It's on the house," Cheyenne said, finishing the last of her beer.

Stoner and I headed for the door.

"Be careful out there, Flynn," she added with a playful salute.

Chapter Four

Arlo Stoner stepped off the old cement pier into a wide-bottomed aluminum boat. It looked like a sixteen-footer. There was a white insulated box about the size of a case of beer behind the center seat, no doubt the snails bound for *La Mouche Noire*.

"Toss me your gear, grab that line, and get in." Stoner yanked the motor's cord just once. The outboard sprang to life in a cloud of oil-drenched smoke. I grabbed the bow line and climbed onto the front seat. We roared away from the pier. A black cloud bank was racing toward Loon Landing from the west. The wind had picked up, too. I had to grab the sides of the boat to keep my seat as we bounced from one wave to the next. Stoner scanned the water as we passed the islands.

"They logged this off back in the twenties, before they built the dam, which created the lake," Stoner shouted over the drone of the motor. "Full of stumps. When the water level's low, like this time of year, you can rip off a prop real easy."

With my back to the bow, I was mostly spared the icy shower that was raining over Stoner face first. He appeared oblivious to the soaking he was getting.

"This is all state land," he shouted with the wave of his hand.

The shoreline was a mix of khaki-toned sand beaches and dense stands of hemlock, yellow birch and maple. The rotted stumps of hundreds of long-logged trees rose like the remains of some ancient parapet from the black muck that marked the lake's low water line. Stoner weaved the boat between two boulders that emerged from the ink-black water like

19

mountainous eggs. Each was more than twenty feet high and splattered with the chalk-white excrement of the screeching gulls we'd driven from their granite roost.

"The lake's bigger than I thought," I shouted.

"The map back there says ten, but it's closer to twelve miles long," Stoner said. "Maybe a mile wide, at the widest…more than a hundred miles of shoreline, what with all the bays and backwater," he added.

"And this is the only way to get to Lost Pond, by boat?" I asked.

"Yup," Stoner replied. "Or snowmobile in the winter. There's a trail, from Black Bear Lake, but that's an eight-mile hike. Railroad shut down in the early sixties, but Cyrus Black—he runs the hotel and general store—Cyrus has a truck that runs on the rails. That's how we get supplies, until winter that is."

"What happens then?" I asked.

"Snowmobile…sled everything in from the Landing. That's an eagle up there," Stoner added, pointing over my shoulder. "We've had a nesting pair here for a couple of years."

I turned and watched it cruising lazily over the lake. Despite what appeared as a coming environmental apocalypse, the re-introduction of the eagle has been a heroic, albeit isolated, success story.

The lake had widened. The shoreline was now barely visible. The dark clouds we'd left behind were now sweeping over us. We rode on, each of us lost in our own thoughts.

"Your grandfather was a good man," Stoner said, breaking a long silence. "We tipped a few."

I was staring over Stoner's shoulder, watching the boat's milky-white wake melt into the waves breaking behind us. I was wishing I'd taken the time to tip a few with him myself.

Stoner was changing course. I looked up. We were rounding a hook-shaped point, mostly rocks and driftwood, a natural barrier against the prevailing west wind.

Then I burst out laughing. We were passing a beaver lodge. Protruding from its roof of sticks and mud was a satellite TV dish.

"That IS funny!" I shouted.

"Somebody put it there a few days ago," Stoner said. "Where else but Lost Pond, know what I mean?"

No, I didn't know, but I was sure I was about to find out.

A misting drizzle was now rolling in wispy sheets over the lake. I grabbed my rain jacket from my duffle and pulled it over me. A kingfisher dove into the water just off the point. It emerged with a wiggling fish and vanished into a thickening icy fog. I wiped my running nose with my sleeve and stared back into the boat's wake that rolled out over the water behind us.

■   ■   ■

The change of the motor's pitch woke me from a dreamy daze. We were slowing down. I looked at Stoner. Rivulets of water were dripping from his tawny beard as if it was a sopped sponge.

"Lost Pond's just ahead," he said.

I turned over my shoulder. There was a long, wood-planked dock emerging out of the milk-thick mist. Several small boats were tied off to either side. We squeezed between two craggy tree stumps.

"Like I said...gets a little tricky this time of year," Stoner said as he shut off the motor and raised the prop.

We slid toward the dock through water barely a foot deep.

The shore was lined with towering pines, some bent in

21

grotesque shapes by the savage winds that ripped up the lake from the northwest.

"Where's the town?" I asked.

"About a quarter mile," Stoner replied, grabbing hold of the dock. He hopped out and tied off the bow line. "Hand me those snails."

I slid the insulated box onto the planking, grabbed my duffle bag, and followed Stoner through the trees to a small dirt parking lot.

"I thought you couldn't drive here?" I asked. There were three rust-ravaged pickup trucks parked under a sagging beech tree.

"You can't," Stoner replied.

Then I noticed that none had license plates.

"We bring 'em out on a barge." Stoner added. He put the snails into the bed of a seventies vintage Ford that looked like someone had smashed every inch of it with a sledge hammer. The truck had been repainted in two shades of blue, probably with a wide bristle brush. It sagged to one side on what was surely a broken spring. The left front tire was nearly flat.

"Toss in your gear."

I threw my duffle onto a pile of empty beer and soda cans. Stoner yanked at the driver's side door, wrenching it from its rusted hinges.

"Climb in and slide over," he said. "The other door's pretty well shot."

The floor of the truck had mostly rotted away. Stoner started the engine. The cab immediately filled with lung-searing smoke.

"Not to worry," he laughed. "The Major's good for another hundred miles. Here that's an eternity."

"The Major?" I asked.

"Bought it for a hundred bucks from an old timer named

22

Major…used it to haul firewood and garbage around the Buzz Point Club on Antler Lake."

Stoner ground the truck into first gear. We lurched forward. The old Ford shook as if it might fall apart around us.

"Not exactly a vintage Corvette," Stoner quipped, "but better suited to the task at hand."

We chugged through a stand of white paper birch and onto a wide, flat meadow thick with golden rod, asters and milkweed. Something leapt into the air and then disappeared back into the waist-high grass.

"What was that?" I asked.

"Coyote," Stoner replied, "eating grasshoppers. Coyote will eat anything. The grasshoppers are just an afternoon appetizer," he added.

I wondered how much further we had to go; The Major was bubbling over like Old Faithful.

"What exactly is the story on this place?" I asked.

"Lost Pond?" Stoner replied, jamming the wheezing truck into third gear. We sputtered across the meadow.

"Began as a logging camp in the early nineteen hundreds. When the loggers cleared out, the railroad bought up everything, built a hotel, depot, support structures. Called it Mohawk Station."

He ground down to second gear, slowing just enough to swerve around a gaping rut in the road.

"The railroad figured to develop its holdings around the lake. But its owner blew his brains out just before the depression. The railroad was sold…a couple of times. The grand scheme never worked out. When the trains stopped running, William and Marshall College bought the whole shebang for pennies on the dollar."

"What did a college want with it?" I asked.

"They turned it into a retreat, conference center, that sort of thing," Stoner continued. "Restored the old hotel and buildings, most of which have been designated historic landmarks. The loggers had always called the place Lost Pond, so the college went back to the original name."

Stoner jammed the truck back up to third gear.

"The conference center never worked out, too far off the beaten path for the seminar-retreat crowd. So in the early seventies the college leased all of Lost Pond to the Friends."

"The who?" I asked

"The Friends of George I. Gurdjieff. It's a commune of artists, craftspeople."

"And these people live out here year 'round?" I asked.

"Most of 'em—Doc Ingram, Black and his wife, several others…maybe three dozen people in all."

"What keeps Lost Pond going, economically?" I asked.

"Summer tourist business, mostly," Stoner replied. "Cyrus Black runs a ferry service between Lost Pond and the Landing. Once the tourists are here, they're kind of a captive audience," he added with a laugh. "And the Friends sell their work at craft fairs in Albany, Syracuse, Buffalo, and in stores around the Park…at least for now," he added.

"What do you mean, for now?" I asked.

"The college is in a financial bind. The trustees have voted to sell their Adirondack holdings. Word is they may already have a buyer lined up…probably some developer…too bad."

Stoner manhandled his truck around a sharp left hand turn. We bounced over the rusted rails of the abandoned railroad.

WELCOME TO LOST POND
ONCE YOU'VE BEEN BITTEN YOU'LL
BE BACK

24

The sign was a stunner, hanging from two pine poles. The letters were hand-carved, painted gold and mounted against a green background. But the sign's focal point was a cartoon-styled black fly, wearing a felt hat, waders, and casting a fly rod.

"You've got to be kidding me," I said.

"The sign was your grandfather's creation," Stoner said. "We've got hats, T-shirts, sweaters. People send us pictures from all over the world decked out in their Lost Pond stuff. Rufus put us on the map," Stoner laughed.

We rumbled through a cluster of wood-frame buildings.

"Is that the French restaurant?" I asked.

It was a single story building painted jet-black. The windows were trimmed in bright yellow. There was a matching yellow awning that covered a small porch with half a dozen round wood tables. A dark-skinned man with a sharply pointed black beard was sweeping the walkway. Stoner honked. The man waved.

"That's my partner, Hakeem Morel," Stoner said. "And that IS the world-famous *La Mouche Noire*."

"The Black Fly. Cheyenne Levine told me about it," I replied. "I still can't believe there's a French restaurant out here in the middle of...nothing."

"Don't sell us short there, mister city slicker," Stoner replied. "Our little slice of heaven is filled with surprises. The bookstore across the street?"

I couldn't quite read the sign in the front yard of a two-story white frame house as we rumbled by.

"The art of what?" I asked

"*The Art of Living*," Stoner replied. "Not your...usual store."

I took the bait that the wily guide had so deftly wiggled past my nose. "What do you mean, not your usual store?"

"You can pick up a *New York Times* bestseller, a bottle of

single malt Scotch or a fine cigar, buy a painting or take an art lesson, all in one stop," Stoner replied. "Megan's quite the entrepreneur."

"Megan?" I asked.

"Megan Seagar," Stoner replied. "She was a teacher in Syracuse. Moved up here a couple of years ago…joined the Friends and opened her store. Damn fine artist…and a good looker," Stoner added with a sly wink I thought a bit appreciative for an allegedly gay man.

"That's Royal Wulff's fly shop next door," Stoner continued. It was a one-story log structure with a lighted SAGE Fly Rods sign hanging in a dust-coated front window. "Royal has probably tied more flies than any man alive," Stoner continued. "You like to fish with flies?"

"I used to, with my grandfather," I replied. "But that was a long time ago."

"Still some damn good trout waters up here," Stoner said. "If you have time, I'll show you some of my secret spots."

I just nodded. I didn't want to tell him I'd be out of Lost Pond in a couple of days.

The road took a hard right. We rumbled over a narrow wood bridge, crossing a fast-flowing, boulder-strewn stream.

"That's Mohawk Lodge," Stoner said, pointing to a sprawling, bark-sheathed structure just visible through a stand of white pine.

"It's right out of the nineteenth century," I said.

A wide porch, supported by massive wood columns, commanded a breath-taking view of the lake.

"Make sure to stick your nose in there before you leave," Stoner added. "It's right out of an Adirondack history book."

The road took a sweeping left-hand turn. We bounced past two log buildings separated by a maple-shaded stone patio. A vegetable garden was prospering in one corner of a sun-drenched meadow carved from surrounding woods.

"That's the commune," Stoner began. "Those log buildings are the real deal, built by lumberjacks a century ago. The one on the right is the kitchen, dining hall and meeting center. The other's the craft center, where everyone works. The Friends' dormitory is on the other side of the trees."

The road dipped back into the woods. We passed the driveways to several lakeside camps. Each was marked with its own distinctive sign: Whitetail Camp; Mountain Rest; Bears' Den; Osprey View. The road ended abruptly at a rippling brook. A yellow wood sign was nailed to a yellow birch hanging over the last driveway:

RUFUS FLYNN

WHERE THE ROAD ENDS AND A GOOD TIME BEGINS.

"Here at last," Stoner said. He pulled down a weedy driveway, The Major coughing and spitting its way through a mix of hardwoods and spruce. Pop's camp was no cabin at all. It was a small house with board and batten siding and painted light yellow. There was a sunroom built off the southwest side. Its ample windows opened to a wildflower garden. Stoner switched off the ignition. The smoking motor gasped twice, and then mercifully expired, perhaps for good. I grabbed my duffle and we headed up the steps.

"I don't have a key," I said.

"Neither did Rufus," Stoner replied, swinging open the door.

The sunroom was paneled in knotty pine. There was a round oak table and four captain's chairs. A beige leather couch was flanked by two end tables with driftwood lamps and birchbark shades. The maple coffee table was carved in the shape of a fish. A wood stove occupied the far corner of the room. The walls were adorned with oil and watercolor Adirondack landscape paintings.

The air inside the house was cold and damp.

The kitchen, just off the sunroom, was small but functional. The cabinets were trimmed with birch bark. There was a wide window that overlooked a modest garden pond.

We walked into Pop's den. The walls were paneled in gray washed pine. The bookshelves were well-stocked, embracing a stone-faced fireplace. There was a black leather couch on one side of the room. My grandfather's reading chair was on the other. It faced the fireplace. Pop's humidor was strategically placed on a table of yellow birch, within easy reach from his chair. I took a look inside. There was an ample selection of Cohibas, Bolivars and Montecristos. All contraband Cuban cigars that Pop smuggled regularly out of nearby Canada. When he had been so moved, he'd send me two or three with his usual note:

"Life is too short to smoke cheap cigars."

A pair of sliding glass doors opened to a sprawling, two-level deck. Pop's study was off the den. Its birch-paneled walls were lined with more books. He'd placed his roll-top cherry desk by a bay window where he could look out over the lake. The desk was open. There were two catalog-sized 10 by 13 envelopes inside. Pop had written my name on both with a black, wide-tipped felt pen. I picked one up for a moment, but placed it almost immediately back on the desk. I wasn't ready for whatever he'd left behind for me.

Stoner was getting a fire started. "I'm going to miss old Rufus," he said, striking a wood match against a slab of granite. The tinder kindling burst into flame. "Thought a fire might cheer the place up a little."

I walked back into the kitchen and checked out the refrigerator. It was pretty much empty, but for an open Genesee Beer twelve-pack, mustard and mayonnaise, and some leftovers in plastic containers.

"What are my dining choices?" I asked Stoner, who'd joined me in the kitchen.

"Hakeem is open 'til nine, he replied. "You can eat at the Friends' dining hall. It's all fresh homemade food, and the price is right. But bring your favorite beverage. Or you can buy some groceries at the Lodge store and cook for yourself."

"I'll start with Hakeem's," I replied, searching through the kitchen cabinets.

"To the right of the stove," Stoner said, knowing I was looking for Pop's booze. I found a bottle of Canadian Club, one of Knob Creek bourbon and several bottles of French white and red wine.

"Knob Creek," Stoner said. "No ice."

"Where can I find this Doc Ingram?" I asked.

Stoner looked at his watch.

"*La Mouche Noire,* in precisely one hour."

"How do you know that?" I asked.

Stoner took a sip of his bourbon. "He's always there...always at five."

I poured three fingers of Canadian Club over a handful of ice cubes. We walked back into the den where I fell into Pop's chair. The whiskey tasted more than good. The fire was already squeezing the cold from the room. I breathed deeply. I'd missed the smell of wood smoke.

"I don't get it."

"Get what?" Stoner asked.

"My grandfather's death," I replied. "The last time I

talked with him he was fine. And this Doc Ingram never told me how he died."

Stoner took a sip from his drink and added a couple of chunks of beech to the fire. I took another swallow. The whiskey was warming me just as quickly as the flaming logs.

"I heard it was a heart attack," Stoner said.

He quaffed down his bourbon and headed for the door.

"Thanks for the drink. Welcome to Lost Pond."

Chapter Five

I unpacked my duffle and made a list of grocery items I thought I'd need for no more than three days. I didn't expect it would take me any longer to clean up Pop's affairs. After restocking the refrigerator, I'd walk over to this French restaurant. If Stoner was right, Doc Ingram would be there. It was about four-thirty. I headed for the grocery store.

The forest takes on a magical aroma in the fall. I drew a deep breath, inhaling a sweet stew of smells—cinnamon, apple and brown sugar—spiced to perfection with wisps of wood smoke. The wind stirred an old maple by the edge of the road. A shower of crimson leaves rained down over me, washing away, for the moment, the disappointments I'd carried with me from the city.

Mohawk Lodge, its siding crafted of spruce slabs with the bark left on, was built in the style of the great camps of the Adirondacks. Its massive front porch was well accommodated with stick wood tables and chairs. The windows were trimmed in yellow birch. Chimney smoke was drifting in thin plumes from the lodge roof and out over the lake.

The grocery store was located on the basement level on the north side of the building. A tinkling bell attached to the top of a worn plank wood door signaled my arrival. But there was no one around. The store was small by any standard. A six-door cooler took up most of one wall. There were four short narrow aisles of canned and packaged goods, a modest produce section and a small checkout counter. I quickly found some bread, eggs and bacon, orange juice, milk, a can of coffee, and packages of sliced turkey and smoked ham. I put

31

everything on the counter by the cash register and waited. Ten minutes passed. When no one appeared I climbed the stairs to the first floor. The living room of the lodge was spacious and warm, anchored by a gigantic stone fireplace large enough to burn logs the length of my leg. And it was doing so with clear efficiency. The floor was made of wide pine boards, partially covered with throw rugs of various southwestern Indian styles. The sidewalls were knotty pine. Adirondack-style rockers and stuffed chairs were arranged in a semi-circle in front of the fireplace. A man and woman perhaps in their early thirties were enjoying a cocktail by the fire.

"Anyone around," I asked, "or are the groceries free?"

"Margo's working out in the den," the man replied, pointing toward the back of the building.

I made my way down a long, narrow pine-paneled hallway. It smelled of fresh stain. A muscular, blonde-haired woman was spinning furiously on an exercise bike in a book-lined room at the end of the hall. She was wearing a headset, listening to music, I assumed, and reading a book. Margo was clearly a skilled multi-tasker.

"Can I help you?" she shouted over the whine of the bike and her music.

"I need to pay for some groceries," I replied.

She looked at her watch. "Two more minutes."

I guessed her to be in her fifties. She'd been pedaling for a while; she was sopping wet. I wandered back out into the hall.

"Looking for something?" He was a lean, rawboned man of medium height, probably in his mid-seventies. His snow-white hair was swept back in a pony tail. A turquoise turtle earring dangled from his left ear. He had a paintbrush in one hand, a plastic bucket in the other.

"I need some groceries. Someone said to see Margo. I

guess that's her?"

"That's Margo, she's my wife," the man replied. "I'm Cyrus Black."

We shook hands. His palm was dry and callused

"I'm sorry about your grandfather," Black said. "If there's anything we can do to help."

"Thanks," I replied. "I need a day or two to sort things out."

Margo bounded out of the den.

"Sorry to keep you waiting," she gasped, still catching her breath. "I gotta keep the old bod in shape."

She kissed her husband warmly on the lips. He patted her shapely behind.

"Know the secret to a long life?" Black asked.

He didn't wait for my reply.

"A young wife."

He winked at me with a mischievous smile. Margo kissed him again, only this time she lingered a bit longer. I wondered what magical aphrodisiac might be bubbling up in the springs around Lost Pond. Cyrus Black withdrew reluctantly and introduced me to his rambunctious wife. She wiped the sweat from her wide brown eyes with the sleeve of her green Mohawk Lodge sweatshirt.

"I'm sorry about Rufus," she said. "He was such a wonderful man. He taught me to play chess. We played every Thursday."

I wondered what else Pop might have taught her...or her him?

"Mr. Flynn needs some groceries," Cyrus Black added hastily. He headed back up the hall with his bucket and brush.

I followed Margo down the stairs, thinking what a marvelous time Pop must have had on Thursdays.

"Your grandfather was working on a book."

"What was it about?" I asked

"I have no idea," Margo replied. "He was doing a lot of research, local Adirondack history, that sort of thing."

She finished ringing up my groceries.

"That'll be $27.58. He didn't say a whole lot about it to me, only that he was getting closer every day, whatever that meant," she added. "Doc Ingram might know more. They were pretty tight. Have you met him yet?"

"He's next on my list."

"Doc won't be hard to find." Like Stoner, she looked at her watch. "He's probably at Hakeem's right now."

"That's what Arlo said," I replied.

■　　■　　■

I put away the groceries, added a couple of large, slow-burning logs to the fire and headed for *La Mouche Noire*. I couldn't wait to see the place. A gourmet French restaurant miles from the nearest road? I still couldn't believe it, but nothing in Lost Pond should have surprised me given Pop's love of eccentric characters and oddball lifestyles.

The sun was sliding below the horizon in fiery plumes of purple and pink. I was glad I'd grabbed my fleece. It would be a cold walk back to the cabin. I was near the top of the driveway when a doe and her fawn burst from a thicket of spruce. The doe bounded down the road, her offspring struggling to keep pace on the loose stones. Then the doe cut sharply to her left. While I was watching the deer disappear into the woods, a raucous blue jay erupted from the pines.

Eeef...eeef...eeef.

It flew off in the general direction of the deer. Alarmed by the jay's warning, a pair of black squirrels abandoned their search for beechnuts and dashed beneath the broken branches of a fallen white pine. I wondered why my presence had so disturbed the natural order of things. But it wasn't me.

Womp...womp...womp.

It was a helicopter, approaching fast and flying low. There was nowhere for me to run. I dropped to my knees, burying my head between my legs. The helicopter was over me an instant later. The roar of the engine pounded my eardrums 'til I thought they would bleed. And then it was gone.

Jesus Christ, who in hell was that?

I staggered to my feet, gagging in the choking dust and debris churned up by the chopper's whirling blades. I wondered what crazy bastard would be flying so low over the lodge, the camps and the commune. But it was clear this wasn't the intruder's first visit. The animals had known what was coming. That's why they'd taken cover.

"Son of a bitch," I mumbled, still cleaning myself off. I continued up the road.

Ten minutes later I walked onto the porch at *La Mouche Noire*. The man and woman I'd seen at the lodge were there, huddled under a hissing gas heater. They'd been joined by another couple. All were wearing heavy sweaters, determined to dine in the great outdoors despite the plummeting temperature. They were sharing a laugh over what was a probably an over-priced bottle of wine. I said hello and ducked inside.

La Mouche Noire was small. There were just six tables, each with a checkered black and yellow tablecloth and a single candle. The walls were painted a soft yellow and decorated sporadically with French impressionist art. But for an elderly man in a wheelchair and a blonde-haired woman, perhaps his daughter, the dining room was empty. The bar was part of the same room, separated by a shoulder-high birch partition topped with potted flowers. A massive mural—an Adirondack lake scene—covered the entire wall behind the bar. The liquor selection, displayed to the left of the cash register, was small, but adequately represented only the best brands. A spry man wearing a navy blue turtleneck sweater was seated at one of the bar's six stools. He was mostly bald, but for tufts of white hair bunched like gobs of cotton around his ears. His yellowish gray moustache was thick but neatly clipped. He had a round, pumpkin-shaped head and the copper nose of a hard-drinking man. He was sipping a martini. It was dressed with three large green olives skewered on a toothpick the size of railroad spike.

"You must be Flynn," the man said in a throaty yet assuredly friendly voice, his vivid green eyes having already swept over me. I must have passed his inspection.

"I'm Ingram." He tipped his mostly empty glass my way. "Welcome to the end of the road."

We shook hands.

"What are you drinking?" he asked, already up and walking behind the bar. "Sandy's out back having a smoke."

I assumed Sandy was the bartender.

"That looks pretty good," I replied, pointing to his glass.

"Bombay Sapphire, dry, with three jalapeno-stuffed olives?"

"Not sure about the jalapenos, but what the hell," I replied.

While Ingram was mixing my drink I took a U.S. Grant from my wallet and put it on the bar.

"The first one's on me," Ingram said, handing me a chilled glass filled to the rim. He returned to his bar stool. "To Rufus," he said, lifting his glass. "He was one hell of a man...a damn good friend."

Ingram mixed a hell of a martini.

"I'll start sorting through my grandfather's stuff tomorrow, who knows what I'll find," I replied. I was hoping Ingram would begin where he'd left off when he'd called me. He said nothing, but took a long sip from his drink. I tried again.

"When you called you said we had more to talk about," I said, sliding an olive off its skewer with my teeth. "How did my grandfather die, and where is his body?"

Ingram put down his glass. "Your grandfather had pancreatic cancer."

Hakeem came out of the kitchen carrying two plates. He served the couple in the dining room, then made his way to the bar.

"Ah, Monsieur Flynn?"

Everyone in Lost Pond must have known I was coming.

He wiped his long fingers on his crisp white apron. We shook hands. His lively black eyes sparkled like opals against his light brown skin.

"I see zee good doctor has welcomed you properly. Please, you are my guest for dinner."

"That's not necessary," I replied.

"I insist," he replied, picking up my fifty and stuffing it in my shirt pocket. Then he rushed off toward the kitchen. "Monsieur Doc, take care of our very special guest!"

I took another sip from the martini. It was going down too easy. "Stoner told me he and Hakeem are...partners," I asked.

Ingram looked at me over the rim of his glasses.

"Cheyenne, back at the landing, she told me they were partners, too, but the way she said it...know what I'm talking about, Doc?"

Ingram plucked an olive from his martini and simply shrugged.

"Hakeem!" the blond-haired woman shouted. "The tuna

tartar…the mango, avocado and green apples…magnificent!"

"That's Tasha, Royal Wulff's wife. He's the guy in the wheelchair," Ingram said. "Old Royal met her on the Internet, brought her over from Bosnia. They were married here three years ago."

"She could be his daughter," I stammered.

"Tasha's twenty-six, Royal is seventy-five," Ingram replied.

I downed the last of my martini. "You're joking."

"Young wife keeps a man young," Ingram said.

"That's what Cyrus Black told me," I replied. "I met Margo. Is there something in the water up here? We could bottle it and make a fortune."

Ingram chuckled. "Let's have another drink." He looked around. "Sandy must be smoking the whole goddamned pack," he added, stepping behind the bar.

"Royal Wulff's the guy with the fly shop across the street, right?" I asked. "Stoner pointed it out to me."

"That's him," Ingram replied as he mixed our martinis. "Royal was quite a guide in his day, before his accident."

"Accident?" I asked.

"Five years ago," Ingram began. "Old Royal said he was…how did he put it…*over-served* at the Tumble Inn. It was near midnight when he headed up the lake in his boat. He ran head-on into the rocks at Indian Shoals. No one found him until morning. Lucky son-of-a-bitch…I guess," Ingram continued. "Now Stoner does the guiding and Royal mainly ties flies, sells them all over the world, thanks to Al Gore."

"Al Gore?" I asked.

"He invented the Internet, didn't he?" Ingram added with a smile.

Hakeem came out of the kitchen wheeling a cart with several plates of steaming mussels. He smiled on his way to the porch.

"How about you, Doc…married?"

"Four times," he replied. He handed me a fresh martini and took a long sip from his own. "You'd think I'd have learned my lesson after the first two, but I kept going back for more…a real masochist." He plucked an olive from his drink. "And you?"

"Married? Came close, once," I replied, sparing him the messy details about Stephanie and me.

"Rufus told me you were some kind of financial genius?" Ingram asked.

I described my current state of affairs in as few words as possible. I wanted to know more about my grandfather's death. But I also wanted to know more about Ingram, and while he was talking, why not let him talk.

"What about you, Doc?" I asked.

"Cardiology, in Dallas mostly."

"How did you end up here, at the end of the road, as you put it?" I asked.

"That's a long story."

"We're not going anywhere."

Ingram took a sip from his drink. "I was hunting in Wyoming—antelope—with an old friend, six, seven years ago. We walked back to the truck after scoping a small herd. The guide, hell, he was just a kid, wanted to move on. I began unloading my rifle but the guide insisted I keep it loaded. 'We hunt Wyoming style,' he said. 'Never know when you might get a shot.' My friend got in the back of the truck with two loaded rifles. We started off, truck hit a rock or something. My rifle went off…put a two-seventy slug through the guide's chest, just above his heart. I was able to keep him alive. We called in a chopper and got him to a hospital. I saved the son-of-a-bitch's life, but he and his family sued me anyway. I was tied up in court for two years. I eventually won. About the same time, wife number four and I called it quits. After the whole mess, I just said the hell with it. I closed my practice, bought a camper and took off. Ever read *Blue Highways*, by William Least Heat Moon?" Ingram asked.

"Never heard of it," I replied.

"Moon had this old van, called it 'Ghost Dancing.' He drove around the country on nothing but back roads, the ones that are marked blue on most maps. I did the same thing. Found myself in Lost Pond five years ago...been here ever since. I tend to the Friends' medical needs...do a little pottery work. It's a good life...good and simple."

"So you live out here year 'round?"

"Yup," Ingram replied, taking a long sip from his drink.

"Where's your place, your camp?" I asked.

"You passed it on the way to your grandfather's, Whitetail Camp. It's been called that since it was built back in the forties."

"If the college owns all this, do they own the camps, too? And how do these Friends connect to all this?" I asked.

"Friends of George I. Gurdjieff," Ingram replied. "William and Marshall College owns everything, but leases it all to the Friends, who sub-lease the camps to your grandfather, Jim Tyler, Wes Duncan and me."

"Who are Tyler and Duncan?" I asked.

"Jim Tyler's a bird carver. Wes Duncan is a photographer. They're here summers only, usually gone by Labor Day," Ingram replied.

"What about Mohawk Lodge?" I asked. "Who owns that?"

"Same deal," Ingram replied. "Cyrus Black and Margo are the managers. We all have one thing in common," he continued. "We all share the same values and beliefs...simple living, working with our hands, that sort of thing."

I snared another olive. "We got a little off the subject. You said my grandfather had cancer of the pancreas?"

Ingram took a long swallow from his martini. "Rufus was diagnosed about six months ago, in Syracuse. There are new drugs, treatments they wanted to try, but purely experimental. Your grandfather said the hell with it...said he didn't want to piss his money away just to hang on a few more weeks or months, maybe. He didn't want to die in a hospice bed somewhere either. He wanted to die here, and on his own terms."

"I'm a little confused," I replied. "How exactly did he die...on his own terms?"

Ingram put down his drink.

"I killed him."

■　　■　　■

I staggered back to Pop's camp. A light snow was falling. I was freezing my ass off, having left my fleece hanging off the back of one of Hakeem's bar stools. Over a dinner of roasted pike perch with braised cabbage and a bottle of Pouilly-Fumé, Doc Ingram had told me everything. Doc hadn't exactly killed my grandfather; he'd hastened his death—by cardiac arrest—with an injection of the barbiturate thiopental. It was euthanasia, pure and simple. Apparently Pop had thrown a hell of a party the day he died. Of course, no one in Lost Pond knew what the party was all about, no one but Doc and Megan Seagar. Cheyenne Levine had provided a keg of Genny draught. A pig was roasted. There was fresh corn on the cob, red-skin potatoes and spinach salad, all from the Friends' gardens. And Pop had savored his favorite for dessert—warm pumpkin pie topped with vanilla ice cream.

Cheyenne had also brought along her fiddle and provided spirited accompaniment for the square dance that followed. About midnight my grandfather said goodbye to everyone and walked back to his camp. Doc and Megan Seagar met him there a few minutes later. They drank some bourbon. Pop smoked his last Cuban. Then Doc gave him the shot. Pop said goodbye, closed his eyes, and was dead a few minutes later. The cover story was that Doc stopped by to have nightcap with my grandfather and had found him dead. The body had been taken to Watertown. Doc had signed the death certificate. Cause of death: cardiac arrest. In New York state, Ingram could go to prison for murder; Seagar, too, as an accomplice, if the truth ever came out.

I wondered if anyone would ever love me enough to commit murder.

At Pop's request, he'd been cremated.

"Where are my grandfather's ashes?" I'd asked.

"You passed him on your way out here today," Doc had replied, pausing for maximum effect. "The beaver lodge, with the TV satellite dish?" he'd said at last.

"You're shitting me," I'd mumbled.

"His ashes are inside. The dish was your grandfather's idea...said he didn't want to miss a Yankees game."

"Jesus Christ," I'd replied. And then I'd laughed my ass off.

Somewhere between Hakeem's pineapple sorbet and a second cup of coffee, I'd gotten around to asking Doc about the novel that Pop was allegedly working on. The book, Doc assured me, was well under way, tracing the lives of six generations of Adirondackers. Pop had completed several chapters when he'd gotten sidetracked, as Doc had put it. Researching the history of early North Country railroads, Pop had come across the suicide of an Adirondack rail baron named Erik von Koenig in 1928. Doc told me that just weeks before setting fire to his mansion—not far from Lost Pond—and taking his life, von Koenig had swindled millions from the investors in his Adirondack Railway and Steamship Company. It was also believed that von Koenig had murdered a trusted associate, a man named Aharon Friedman, before setting the fire and then blowing his own brains out with a German Lugar pistol. What captivated my grandfather, Doc had said, was that the money von Koenig had stolen from his investors—as well as his personal fortune—had simply vanished. And von Koenig's motives—for embezzlement, murder, and suicide—had remained a mystery for nearly a century. Doc told me that Pop had spent the last year of his life attempting to unravel the von Koenig saga.

"What did my grandfather find out?" I'd asked Doc.

"Everything is in the envelope, on his desk," Doc had replied. "The rest is up to you."

I'd made it to the top of Pop's driveway. The eerie wail of a loon rolled across the lake. It was a youngster, no doubt, left behind by its parents. They'd already departed for the Carolinas. The loon would have to find its way on its own.

I felt pretty much on my own as well.

■　　■　　■

There wasn't much left in the fireplace other than smoldering embers. I found some stick wood and stoked the fire back to life. Pop's electric power came from the Friends' generator. Stoner had told me it was shut down nightly at eleven. Lights were then powered by a bank of batteries stored just off Pop's kitchen. But there were also propane lights in the living room and in the study. I lit those, preferring their comforting glow to the glare of city bulbs. I warmed myself by the fire for a few minutes and then reached into the humidor. I clipped off a Cohiba, struck a wood match against the fireplace, and settled into my grandfather's reclining leather chair. Pop had lived simply, but he'd lived damn well. I took a long draw on the cigar, watching its sweetness drift lazily across the room and disappear into the fire and up the chimney. Would Cuban cigars taste as good if we could buy them at our corner cigar store instead of smuggling them into the country—President John F. Kennedy's Cuban trade embargo having lasted nearly half a century? I took another puff. Damn right they would. I was beginning to feel a little light-headed. Was it Doc Ingram's martinis, the French wine or the forbidden fruit of Cuba's tobacco farmers? Probably a little of each. I found one of Pop's insulated jackets, threw it on and walked out onto the deck. The snow had stopped. Under a full harvest moon, the surface of the lake sparkled as if it had been strung in Christmas lights. A coyote yipped on the far shore. A soft yet bone-chilling breeze stirred a flurry of leaves from the yellow birches surrounding the deck. It was easy to see why Pop loved this place. I sat on the edge of the steps and stared out across the water. I wondered how many times he'd had taken a seat in this very place, what heady thoughts might have rumbled across his non-stop mind? I wished I'd been sitting here with him, at least once or twice, before he'd left me for good.

I finished the cigar and stumbled toward the bedroom. I was probably out cold before my head hit the pillow

Chapter Six

Ratta-tat-tat...ratta-tat-tat tat.

I opened one eye, painfully, then the other. The dials on my watch slowly came into focus. It was just past seven. I rolled to the edge of the bed and squinted out the window. The autumn leaves, a kaleidoscope of yellows, oranges and reds, were speckled across the cerulean sky as if Monet himself had painted them there with a wide bristle brush.

Ratta-tat-tat...ratta-tat-tat.

One furious woodpecker was pounding away at a dead birch with the ear-splitting clamor of a jackhammer. I could still taste the Cohiba, or was it Hakeem's garlic-soaked braised cabbage? Reeling into the bathroom, I twisted the tap open and threw handfuls of icy lake water over my unshaven face. After brushing the remnants of last night's dinner from my teeth, I made for the kitchen and got a pot of coffee started.

"Hello...anyone up yet?"

I checked to make sure my fly was zipped and made for the back door.

"Good morning," I offered. She was a chestnut brunette, maybe five-ten, with wide, warm amber eyes that danced in the morning light. Her face was well tanned, almost the color of maple syrup. She wore faded jeans that accented her shapely, muscular legs, and beneath her red fleece there was the suggestion of a generous bosom. She had a paper bag in one hand and a brushed-aluminum travel mug in the other.

"I'm Megan Seagar. I brought you some blueberry muffins, fresh from the oven."

45

"Well thank you," I replied. "Come in. Let me warm up that coffee."

I found some dishes in the pantry. While she was gazing out the window, I swept the mouse turds from a couple of plates onto the floor. The deck was already splashed in warm sunlight. It seemed as good a place as any to get to know Megan Seagar.

"You're books and booze, right?" I asked, instantly realizing I probably sounded like an asshole.

Luckily, she laughed. "I prefer The Art of Living."

"You should open a bakery, too," I said. "These muffins are delicious."

"I am a bakery," she replied. "To make it in Lost Pond, you have to be a multi-product marketer, or have enough money that you don't need to work at all."

She took a long sip from her coffee and stared out across the bay.

"I loved your grandfather; I mean we were friends." When she turned back to me her eyes glistened with tears.

"Ingram told me about...the end. Thank you for giving my grandfather what he wanted, and for the risk you and Doc are taking," I said. "I don't think I could have done it."

I put my arms around her, kissing her gently on the forehead.

"Thank you."

"After Doc gave him the shot, I had to go outside," she replied. "I didn't want your grandfather to see me cry. I cried all night."

Tears were now pouring down her cheeks.

"I'm sorry," she sobbed, burying her head into my shoulder.

"Doc told me about his final resting place, the beaver lodge," I said, hoping to break the gloom. "Pop did it his way, that's for sure."

She sniffled through a soft laugh. I wiped away her tears with my handkerchief.

"Arlo Stoner told me you were a teacher, in Syracuse," I said, eager to change the subject.

"I taught high school art," she began. "More than half of my students—juniors and seniors—thought art would be a snap elective." She took a sip of her coffee. "Their interest in learning anything about art was zero, zilch. There were discipline issues almost every day, not just in my classes, but throughout the school. When one of our teachers got shoved down a flight of stairs…that was enough for me."

"A real blackboard jungle," I offered.

"I wanted to be a teacher since I was seven years old. Maybe I was just in the wrong place at the wrong time…maybe I'll go back someday. I just don't know right now."

"How did you end up in Lost Pond?" I asked. "It's pretty far off the beaten path to start a new business."

"That's a fair question," she began. "My uncle was one of the Friends' founders."

"The commune?" I asked.

"That's right. He was a silversmith. I came up here every summer when I was a kid. He passed away three years ago, about the time I decided to take a break from teaching and see if I could make it as an artist. I assumed his lease."

"What exactly is this Friends of George…?" I asked.

Megan smiled. "George I. Gurdjieff."

"That's him," I chuckled.

"Gurdjieff was a Greek Armenian teacher," she continued. "He believed that creative work can lead to a better understanding of the purpose of human life. Gurdjieff was convinced that most men and women live in a virtual trance, using only a fraction of their energy and ability. The Friends was founded on these principals, that we humans could achieve an awakened state through the balanced development of head, hands, and heart. Gurdjieff believed that involvement with merely one's ego was the source of most of our human difficulties."

I polished off my muffin, washing it down with the last of my coffee. "That's a lot to swallow at seven-thirty in the morning."

"Your grandfather was a believer," Megan replied. "Rufus said his writing was like a journey, opening his mind and his eyes to new things, and new ways of seeing things. He said Walt Whitman called it 'the profound lesson of reception.'"

"I guess I never saw that side of him," I admitted. "He invited me up here, more than once, to learn what he'd learned, as he put it. I was just too busy. At least that's what I thought at the time."

"Rufus called you the Financial Genius. What do you do, in the big city?" Megan asked, raising her eyebrows and giving me a wry smile.

"Did," I replied. "Mergers, leverage buyouts, later hedge funds and the futures market. Then subprime mortgages imploded. The investment bank I worked for lost billions. My whole division was wiped out."

"A bummer," Megan replied.

"I'm in good shape. I could get a job tomorrow…if I wanted," I replied. "But I'm not sure I want to go back to that."

I walked to the edge of the deck and looked out over the water.

"Maybe this is just what I need…at least for the time being."

A loon called from across the lake, as if echoing my

sentiments.

"I'm not sure where my life is headed either," Megan said. "I need to focus on my art...and *me* right now."

I wondered what *me* meant. Was Megan Seagar running away from something else besides the classroom—a broken marriage, a relationship gone sour, perhaps?

"Tell me about your art," I asked.

"Watercolors, mostly, Adirondack landscapes," she began. "It takes a while to generate a following. I sell most of my work here and around the Park, Lake Placid, Saranac Lake, Old Forge and Lake George. I've just got a Web site up, and two galleries, one in Rochester and another in Philadelphia, have agreed to carry my work."

"I'm impressed," I offered.

"It's a start, but right now what I sell in the store, the books and booze as you put it, that's paying the bills."

She finished off her coffee.

"I know you've got your hands full, so I'll push off," she said. "Let's take a paddle. I'd love to show you around...and whatever I can do to help," she added.

"Thanks," I replied. "There is one thing...what do you know about this book my grandfather was writing...about some rail baron...a missing fortune?"

She smiled. "I helped your grandfather with his research. He left everything for you on his desk."

"I found it," I replied. "I haven't opened it yet."

"Your grandfather..." Her voice trailed off momentarily. "He hoped you would join us."

"Join us?" I asked. "Join what?"

"It's all there, in the envelope," she replied. "Where we go from here, well, that's going to be up to you," she added as we walked down off the deck.

And I thought I could be back in the City in three days.

49

■   ■   ■

Womp...womp...womp.

It was another helicopter. This time it was sweeping in over the point. It was painted black. There was some kind of insignia on the door, but I couldn't make it out. After gaining elevation, it disappeared behind the ridgeline on the far side of the lake.

"That's the second helicopter I've seen since I got here. Might be the same one," I added.

"That's Simeon Leache, his helicopter anyway," she replied.

"The ex-senator? " I asked.

"Convicted felon and white supremacist," Megan added.

"I catch his radio show once in while, just to see what's got him fired up at the moment," I said. "What's Simeon Leache doing up here?"

"About five years ago, he purchased United Timber's Essex holdings, more than eight thousand acres," she replied. "That's about ten miles to the northeast. I've heard he built his own medieval castle up there, overlooking Fisher Lake, though no one around here's ever seen it."

"What do you mean, never seen it?" I asked.

"It's private, VERY private property, a compound, really. Ever listen to Leache? I mean listen carefully?" Megan asked. "His so-called Institute for the Preservation of American Values? It's a white power movement. If you aren't white, and you're not a Christian, if you or your parents immigrated to the United States, you're not included in what he calls 'The Real America.'"

"Now that you mention it," I replied, "there was a piece in the *Times* a month or so ago suggesting that Leache is secretly funding something called the Aryan Brotherhood. The story linked it with the murders of five immigrant rights activists in Texas and California."

"Leache is investing in more than that," Megan replied. "He's offered William and Marshall College ten million dollars for Lost Pond...all of it."

"Jesus," I replied. "Arlo Stoner told me the college was in financial trouble, and that he thought there might be some deal in the works, but he never mentioned Simeon Leache."

"He wants to build his Institute here," Megan continued, "a school for what he calls a new breed of American patriots. That, of course, will be the end of Lost Pond, possibly the end of the Friends, and the beginning of...well, who knows?"

"But why here?" I asked.

"By helicopter, his compound is minutes from Lost Pond," Meagan replied. "Its isolation will allow Leache to control who comes in and who doesn't. And there's his brother, Crawford."

"His brother?"

"Crawford Leache is Cassiar Industries," Megan continued. "It's based in Marlow, not a hundred miles from here. Cassiar built Leache's compound and they'll no doubt build his institute at Lost Pond."

"Yeh, it's all coming back to me now," I said. "Wasn't it Cassiar's no-bid military contracts that got Simeon Leache kicked out of the U.S. Senate?"

"That's right. Leache should have gone to prison, but his senate colleagues let him simply resign," Megan replied. "He faded away for a while and then reappeared as a born-again Christian, America's self-appointed savior against the terror of diversity. Pardon me while I puke," she added, sticking a long, slender finger down her throat.

"How do you really feel?" I joked.

"Sorry," she replied, "but he's a very bad actor."

"I know Leache is raking in millions, but that's not enough for what you say he's planning to do. There's got to be more to it," I said.

"Your grandfather thought the same thing," Megan replied. "It's all in the papers he left for you. Does the name Vladimir Zubkov mean anything to you?"

"Zubkov is Caspian Energy, Russia's leading oil and natural gas exporter. He's also one of the world's richest men," I replied. "He also has ties to the old KGB and the new Russian mob."

She looked a little surprised.

"I had a client who wanted to invest in Caspian. Did a little research, courtesy of a friend in the CIA. My client put his money elsewhere."

"Your grandfather put it all together," she continued. "Leache and Zubkov have had close ties for years. Cassiar is Caspian Energy's biggest construction contractor. Leache has the money to purchase Lost Pond. But he'll need more, a lot more, to build his so-called institute, to fund his political organization. Your grandfather believed that Zubkov has committed more than fifty million dollars to Leache…but Leache has to purchase Lost Pond first," she added.

"Like I said, it's all there in the papers your grandfather left you," Megan said. "Thanks for the coffee. I'll catch up with you later."

I couldn't take my eyes off her as she walked up the driveway. *Holy shit! What in God's name was I getting into?*

■　　■　　■

There were two bundles of papers inside the envelope. The first included Pop's banking records, investment statements, and his will. He had just under a thousand dollars in his checking account. His bills—propane, telephone, wireless Internet and satellite service—all of which totaled about $210—were fully paid. Surprisingly, he had nearly $750,000 remaining in his IRA account, not bad for a man who'd lost half his net worth in the divorce. I began thumbing through his last will and testament. There was the usual boilerplate about expenses, then a detailed distribution of securities to five environmental organizations. Surprisingly, Megan Seagar was the recipient of $100,000. But the bulk of his estate was left to the Friends of George I. Gurdjieff Society.

Then I saw a crisply folded handwritten note.

September 20, 2007

Dear Ryan:

I'm sorry to have left you this way. You've read my will. I know that you've already made more money than you probably deserve; you won't need any of mine. Besides, I think I've left you something of far greater value. Several months ago I was diagnosed with pancreatic cancer. It was spreading, and the pain grew more intense with every passing day. I sure as hell wasn't going to die in some hospital bed, and I wasn't going to leave Lost Pond to do it. I had a better idea. Doc Ingram or Megan Seagar can fill you in on the details if they haven't already. It was one hell of a party! In the last days of a man's life he looks back on those things from which he received the most joy and satisfaction, and, of course, he wonders what legacy he might leave behind. Some of the best times of my life were the days I spent with you here in the Adirondacks. I know your own life has taken you in other directions. But when you are ready, this cabin will be here for you—if Lost Pond can be saved. Megan and Doc are the only people I've told about my incredible discovery. Before reading further, please study the contents of the second packet before you.

Jesus, Pop. What the hell were you up to?

■   ■   ■

I began by spreading everything out on the floor—newspaper clippings, magazine articles, copies of letters, brittle yellowed photographs, and Pop's nearly unreadable notes and scribbled drawings. Next I organized it all chronologically. The first clipping was from the *Herkimer Daily Telegram*. It was dated November 10, 1928.

Erik von Koenig Found Dead
Fire Guts Eagle's Nest Mansion

Murder-Suicide Suspected in
Mount Lorraine Tragedy

Erik von Koenig, chairman of the Adirondack Railway and Steamship Company, was found dead yesterday in the charred ruins of his mansion at Mount Lorraine.

According to Herkimer County Coroner Wayne Trimble, von Koenig died of a single gunshot wound to the head. The body of Aharon Friedman, von Koenig's company treasurer, was found in the estate's carriage house. Friedman had been shot through the back of his head.

"It appears von Koenig murdered Friedman, set the mansion ablaze, and then took his own life," Herkimer County Sheriff Craig Garrett said.

A German Lugar revolver was found at von Koenig's side. The coroner's office reported it was the same gun that killed Friedman.

"I am stunned," said von Koenig's wife, Lorraine, who was in residence at the family's winter home in West Palm Beach, Florida. "There simply is no explanation for what the police have told me."

Authorities have also reported that Louie LaMont, winter caretaker for von Koenig's Adirondack estate,

54

is missing.

"LaMont is not a suspect, but we'd like to talk to him," said Sheriff Garrett. "He may help us understand von Koenig's frame of mind, what possibly could have driven him to commit murder, then take his own life."

Three photos accompanied the article: von Koenig, a regal-looking figure in formal riding wear, astride a black stallion; Friedman, in horn-rimmed glasses and wearing an eye shade; and the fire-gutted stone mansion.

Pop had circled Friedman's photo. There was a yellow Post-it note attached to the clipping:

"What did Friedman know? What drove von Koenig to kill him?"

There were more clippings. Pop had labeled them *BACKGROUND*. I continued reading, learning that Erik Von Koenig had grown up in the Austrian village of Lambach. There was a photo of the future tycoon singing in a boys' choir at a Catholic Benedictine monastery. There were stories about von Koenig's building of the railroad, its grand opening, early derailments and fires, and von Koenig's plans to develop several lake properties.

The next clipping, dated November 30, 1928, was taped to a piece of white paper.

Millions Missing in Secret Railway Sale

Did Erik von Koenig Swindle Investors?

Investigators have confirmed the mysterious, previously undisclosed sale of the Adirondack Railway and Steamship Company to a South Africa mining consortium—just weeks before the suicide death of the transportation company's founder, Erik von Koenig.

The sale was reportedly completed in early October without the knowledge of the company's board of directors. At about the same time, it has been learned, von Koenig closed on the sale of his Adirondack land holdings. The sale, to a New York City investment group, included more than 500,000 acres of land in the Central Adirondacks of Upstate New York.

"I am shocked and saddened," said Dexter D. Bogart III of Philadelphia, one of von Koenig's largest investors. "There is simply no explanation for the tragedy that has befallen Erik's family and the company."

Rolf Mueller, president of Trans-Afrika Mining Partners, declined to reveal any details of what he said was a private transaction between his company and von Koenig. "The sale was completed in a fully legal manner," Mueller said.

Investigators confirmed that the proceeds from both the sale of von Koenig's company and his vast land holdings—estimated to be in the millions of dollars—have simply vanished.

"We have scoured Erik von Koenig's financial records," said retired New York City police detective Earl Hatcher, who has been retained by von Koenig's widow, Lorraine.

"We are now excavating portions of the Eagle's Nest property. So far we've come up empty. Millions have simply vanished," Hatcher added.

Pop had circled Aharon Friedman and Rolf Mueller, connecting them with a line, and adding a question mark.

I picked up the next clipping; this one was dated December 3, 1928.

Body of von Koenig Caretaker Discovered at Lake Champlain

A body discovered yesterday on the western shore of Lake Champlain about half a mile south of Split Rock Point has been identified as Louie LaMont, caretaker at the Mount Lorraine estate of the late Erik von Koenig.

LaMont has been missing since the bodies of von

Koenig and his company treasurer, Aharon Friedman, were discovered in early November in the charred ruins of von Koenig's central Adirondack mansion. It is believed that von Koenig shot Friedman through the back of his head before setting fire to his mansion and then taking his own life.

"Louie LaMont has never been a suspect in the tragic events at Mount Lorraine," said Herkimer County Sheriff Craig Garrett.

Millions of dollars are also missing from the mysterious sale of von Koenig's Adirondack Railway and Steamship Company and his Adirondack land holdings, estimated to be more than 500,000 acres.

"LaMont might have provided us with a lead that would help unravel this tragic mystery," Garrett said. Investigators have been unable to locate LaMont's wife, Julia, or their son, Jacob. The LaMont cabin at Porcupine Pond was reportedly abandoned a month before von Koenig's death.

Pop had circled Louie LaMont's name and added several questions marks for emphasis.

The last story Pop had filed was dated July 23, 1939. It reported the sale of the Adirondack Railway and Steamship Company by Trans-Afrika Mining to a group of American investors. The same article also reported the sale of von Koenig's previous real estate holding to three national lumber companies. That was it, until the mid-1980s when the magazine *Adirondack Trails* ran a long feature under the headline:

Legend of the Lost von Koenig Treasure

I began reading. There wasn't much I hadn't already learned. But the writer did reveal a journal allegedly kept by a man named Seth Adams, a retired railroad engineer who'd died in 1947. Adams had worked for many years for the Adirondack Railway and Steamship Company. In his journal, Adams had written that on the night of November 3, 1928, he was at the controls of the Canadian Flyer, a Montreal-bound train that made an unscheduled stop at von Koenig's private station, Eagle's Nest, at the foot of Mount Lorraine. Adams had written that he saw an armed man climb aboard his train's caboose. He also wrote that von Koenig himself had handed the man four satchel-sized bags. Adams claimed he'd been told by Aharon Friedman never to reveal that he'd stopped the train at Eagle's Nest that night. Adams had speculated that the mysterious passenger was Louie LaMont, but he couldn't be sure. The magazine's writer noted, however, that the alleged journal had been judged a forgery, perpetrated by Adams' estranged wife to hopefully sell to a book publisher.

Thereafter, Adams' claims were never taken seriously or investigated further. The writer also noted the sale—over a period of years—of von Koenig's previous North Country holdings to the State of New York and their subsequent addition to the Adirondack Park Forest Preserve. The history of von Koenig's railroad was also fleshed out in greater detail, ending with its closing in the early 1960s. It had pretty much been agreed upon, the writer had summarized, that von Koenig's fortune had been lost in the Eagle's Nest blaze. Why had Erik von Koenig swindled millions from his investors, murdered his treasurer, Aharon Friedman, set fire to his mansion and blown his own brains out? The writer hadn't found the answers. The mystery—as of the article's publication—remained unsolved. Almost as a footnote, the writer added that von Koenig's widow, Lorraine, had returned to Germany about a year after her husband's death. She was reportedly killed in an Allied bombing raid over Berlin in late 1944.

The last clipping I found was also cut from the same Adirondack monthly. But the paper was still glossy white. It was dated January-February 2007.

Police ID "Last Hermit of the Adirondacks"

New York State Police have identified the elusive figure until now known only as "The Last Hermit of the Adirondacks." Police say he is Ethan LaMont, a retired U.S. Army major and the grandson of Louis LaMont, a legendary North Country trapper and guide. Louis LaMont was a caretaker for North Country railroad baron Erik von Koenig.

Von Koenig committed suicide in 1928 after stealing millions from his company's investors. Louis LaMont drowned in Lake Champlain shortly after von Koenig's death. The von Koenig's fortune has never been found.

U.S. Army records show that Ethan LaMont is a decorated Vietnam War Green Beret. An Army spokesman said the details of LaMont's military record are classified. LaMont retired from military service in 1994. His whereabouts, until now, were largely unknown.

Popularized by North Country media as "The Last Hermit of the Adirondacks," the ghost-like figure we now know is Ethan LaMont has long been suspected in a series of winter break-ins at isolated Adirondack vacation homes.

Back-country bushwhackers have occasionally stumbled across crude, limb-wood shelters that authorities believe belonged to the Hermit, who over the past decade has reached near-mythical status. Seen only once—when he rescued four Boy Scouts lost in the Five Ponds Wilderness Area—LaMont is described as a bearded, muscular man who moves through the woods like a wisp of smoke.

"We were freezing cold in the rain, our food was gone and Jimmy had a sprained ankle," said Brad Burdett, age 12, of Syracuse. "The Hermit built us a shelter, cooked us a hot meal, dried our clothes, and then led us back to our canoe the next day. He's awesome!"

59

MARK W. HOLDREN

Pop had attached a Post-it note:

Find Ethan LaMont!!

That was it.

Who was supposed to find the so called Last Hermit of the Adirondacks...and why?

I brewed a pot of fresh coffee and returned to Pop's letter.

Are you beginning to connect the dots? Erik von Koenig put a bullet in the back of Aharon Friedman's head because his treasurer had discovered the terrible truth. Friedman had not only uncovered von Koenig's fleecing of his investors, he'd also learned what von Koenig planned to do with his fortune—and he devised a plan to stop him. Aharon Friedman also feared for his life. So he wrote a letter and sent it to be filed with his papers at the University of Berlin. He'd taught there until immigrating to the United States in 1920. Friedman's instructions were that the letter be opened upon his death. But the letter was simply filed away—and remained unread for nearly a century. Suspecting that Friedman was the key to unraveling the von Koenig mystery, I contacted a legal firm in Berlin. They obtained Friedman's papers and sent me his letter. Recognizing its explosive nature, it is not included with these clippings and notes. Here's how you can find it:

Hayduke's Night March

After you've read Friedman's astonishing confession, I have some final thoughts for you. (Are you having fun yet?)

Pop hadn't lost his flair for the dramatic. And he'd already hooked me like a hungry trout. I took my coffee and headed for the den. Hayduke, of course, was George W. Hayduke, the principal character in Edward Abbey's rollicking classic, *The Monkey Wrench Gang*. It was one of Pop's favorite books, one he'd often referred to around our Adirondack campfires. I found his dog-eared copy on the second shelf of the bookcase. I went to the contents...Chapter Seven—Hayduke's Night March. Thumbing through to page 98 I found a small gold key taped to the middle of the page. Looking around, I quickly spotted a gray steel box on the bookshelf. The key fit.

The paper inside had turned brittle with age. The letter was addressed to a Peter Shipman. I assumed he must have been one of Friedman's university colleagues.

October 19, 1928

To my dear friend, Peter:
I hope this letter finds you in good health. I am writing to you as my life may be in imminent danger. If the mission I am about to undertake fails, my friends and colleagues must know that I was not a part of my employer's evil pursuit but in fact gave my life in trying to stop it. Here is my statement. Please file it with my papers—with instructions that it be opened upon my death. Thank you, Peter. May God help us all.
Aharon

My name is Aharon Friedman. I am in the employ of Erik von Koenig and the Adirondack Railway & Steamship Company in the United States of America. The seeds of the conspiracy that I have uncovered were sown more than twenty years ago in Lambach, Austria. Erik von Koenig was born there in 1889. He attended the Benedictine monastery school where he sang in the boys' choir. There he became fast friends with a fellow choirboy with whom von Koenig has corresponded regularly since moving to America with his parents in 1908. With Germany suffering the hardships inflicted upon it in the Great World War, von Koenig's boyhood friend now leads a radical, anti-Semitic political movement that seeks to take control of Germany. Erik von Koenig's boyhood friend is Adolph Hitler. The Nazi leader is seeking von Koenig's financial support, and has urged him to join the Nazi cause. I have recently learned that Erik von Koenig has secretly liquidated his assets—and in the process has stolen millions from his investors—for the sole purpose of financing the final consolidation of Hitler's power over all of Germany. In return, von Koenig will assume a leadership role in Hitler's Nazi movement. Von Koenig believes the American economy will collapse within the year, triggering a world-wide depression. Fearing implosion of the U.S. dollar, he has converted all of his assets to diamonds—lighter and easier to smuggle out of the country than gold or silver bars. These diamonds are scheduled to be transported in just weeks on von Koenig's own train to Montreal. It is von Koenig's intention to escape to Canada and sail to Germany with the diamonds on November 6, 1928. The diamonds must not reach Adolph Hitler! I will give my life, if necessary, to stop this madness. The diamonds will be escorted to Canada by a man named Louie LaMont. He is a courageous and honorable man who has agreed to help me in this gallant cause. LaMont will jump from the train near the Otter River, secrete the diamonds, and then cross Lake Champlain to Vermont. He has already moved his family there, to a cabin near Ferrisburg. I will join him there, after which we will alert the authorities and make arrangements to reimburse the company's investors.

We trust in God's help.

Aharon Friedman
October 19, 1928

I can't remember how long I stared at Friedman's chilling words. I know my coffee was ice cold when I finally put the letter down. Pop had solved the mystery that had baffled North Country investigators, historians and conspiracy buffs for nearly a century. Aharon Friedman and Louie LaMont were heroes. But what did LaMont's grandson Ethan, the so-called Last Hermit of the Adirondacks, have to do with von Koenig's missing diamonds? Why had Pop circled his name and scribbled "*Find Ethan LaMont!!*" on the Post-it note?

I nuked my coffee in the microwave and returned to my grandfather's letter.

Now you've read what's taken me nearly two years to compile —

Aharon Friedman had a keen sense of history. He'd read enough about Adolph Hitler to fear the worst—the Holocaust—and the horrors of a second world war. The diamonds are out there, somewhere between the Otter River trestle and Lake Champlain. My plan—before this damn cancer—was to find Ethan LaMont and enlist his help in finding the diamonds. Your role in my plan, mister financial genius, was to leverage von Koenig's fortune into sufficient funds to exceed Simeon Leache's bid price for Lost Pond.

Holy shit! I read on.

Leache and his followers are counterfeit patriots, wrapping themselves in God and country but ferociously dedicated to building a profit-at-any-cost corporate state—at the expense of the personal freedoms and sacred equal rights of all our citizens. Leache, and Russia's Vladimir Zubkov—who I have discovered is a silent partner in Leache's grand scheme to reshape America—are dangerous men. Doc Ingram and Megan Seagar share my views. They'll help you in any way that they can.

I leave this in your hands, Ryan, trusting you'll do the right thing.

Love, Pop

I needed a walk, some fresh air, time to sort through what my grandfather had left squarely in my lap. Track down some Last Hermit character? Hell, he'd been seen just once, in how many years? And what if I was able to stumble upon Ethan LaMont? What then? If he knew where the diamonds were, he'd have packed them off years ago. And why should he help me find them, if that was even possible? We'd have to scour nearly a thousand square miles. The Hermit would think me mad. I wondered if Doc Ingram and Megan Seagar had really bought into Pop's wild-assed scheme, or if they were simply humoring him, playing along in the last days of his life?

I was ambling up the road from Pop's cabin—heading back toward the lodge—when I discovered a narrow footpath that led off into a thick stand of hemlocks. I was surprised I hadn't seen it before; I took the road less traveled. A blue jay scolded me with a raucous *jeeah...jeeah* for trespassing into its territory. The broad pine boughs—nature's umbrella—kept the trail comfortably cool in the mid-day sun. I'd walked five minutes or so when I found myself at the edge of the Friends' commune.

Clang-clang-clang.

The beating of a hammer on hot metal; the smell of coal smoke drifting from the smithy's forge: I'd found the Friends' workshop. It was a long, one-story log building. The side door was open. I wandered in.

The air was a pungent jambalaya of smoke, wet clay, pinewood shavings, glue and wood stain. In addition to the blacksmith, there was a potter—a gray-haired woman—working at her wheel. A furniture-maker was gluing a pine rocking chair together. He was a small man with the frame of a finch, his head wrapped with a blue-checked bandana.

I ambled down between several long wood tables.

"Hello, may I help you?"

I hadn't seen Oliver Scott when I'd walked in. He had a pair of welder's goggles dangling from his neck.

"Could I get you some tea?" he asked.

Oliver Scott was probably in his early fifties. He was a graceful man with thick gray hair and a beard to match. I followed him to a galley-sized kitchen tucked in one corner of the building. There was a silver cast-iron wood stove, a propane-fired two-burner stove, a small refrigerator and a brushed-steel washing sink. Scott dropped two tea bags into sand-colored stoneware mugs, and then filled them with steaming water from the stove. We sat down at a round, rough-hewn wood table.

■　　　■　　　■

"We'll let it steep a little," he said. "What do you think of Lost Pond, so far?"

"It's Thoreau meets Walt Whitman," I replied.

Scott laughed. "In all of nature, only man asks, 'Why am I here?'"

"And why ARE you here, Oliver Scott?" I asked, immediately wishing I hadn't been quite so intrusive. It was probably none of my business. But Scott didn't seem to mind at all. In fact he seemed to welcome the question.

"This is a more purposeful life than where I came from," he began.

"And that was?" I asked, deciding he wanted to talk.

"I was a personal injury attorney in Boston. Now I am a sculptor, in steel. Living here has opened me to possibilities I never imagined, Ryan. The path to true fulfillment lies in our hands as well as our hearts. This is the core belief that holds the Friends together."

I liked Oliver Scott immediately.

A graceful woman, her ponytail long enough that it touched her willowy waist, joined us in the kitchen. She was carrying a basket of butternut squash. Her name was Molly Hunter. She was the Friends' chief gardener.

"The growing season's got to be pretty short up here," I offered.

"We have a greenhouse to jump-start everything as much as we can," she replied. "And I keep busy the rest of the year," she replied. "I'm a weaver, and I play a mean fiddle," she added with a smile.

"She does indeed," Scott said, handing me my mug of tea while Molly Hunter started one of her own.

"How long have you been here, with the Friends?" I asked, wondering if Hunter was perhaps running from her past as well.

"About two years," she replied. "It's an incredibly powerful place. The rhythm of my work, the energy I feel from the things we grow allows me to listen more closely to what my art can teach me. I've been able to explore parts of me that have nothing to do with how smart I may be." Her lively blue eyes sparkled as she carefully crafted her words.

"Let's take our tea and mosey over to the dining hall. It's about lunch time. You can meet some of the others," Scott offered. "Bring your tea with you."

"See you there," Hunter added. "I have to talk to Willie. He's making new hinges for the barn doors." I assumed Willie was the blacksmith, who was still pounding away at his anvil.

Scott and I walked out into the courtyard. The smell of fresh-baking bread told me we were headed in the right direction.

"We are all searching for a deeper understanding of

ourselves," he began. "Our work here and the values we share as a community generate a remarkable degree of attention to our lives. This leads to a more balanced life and greater inner peace. It will be a terrible shame when all of this is gone."

"You mean if the college sells it," I asked.

"When, not if," Scott replied. "The college is hurting, we all know that. Its board has made the decision to sell Lost Pond. And it looks like Simeon Leache is going to buy it. That's no secret, either. We understand that he'll be here today with Winnie."

"Who is Winnie?" I asked.

"Oh, excuse me," Scott said. "Winnie Stephenson is president of William and Marshall College. I've served as the Friends' liaison to the college the last couple of years. I spoke with her just last week. She told me Leache was bringing one of his green eye shaders with him to look over the lodge's books, give them some idea of what they'll keep, what they'll quite likely tear down. Lost Pond is eligible for the National Register of Historic Places," Scott continued, "but that can't prevent Leache from bulldozing it under." He shook his head. "What a terrible loss it will be."

"I'm still not clear," I asked. "How does Lost Pond...the Friends work, financially, I mean?"

"A portion of everything we make and sell goes back to the Friends, for operating expenses, our lease from the college, marketing costs," Scott began. "That, of course, doesn't cover everything. Hakeem, Royal Wulff and Megan Seagar lease their buildings from the Friends, as do the camp owners, your grandfather included. Oh," he added. "I'm sorry for your loss. Rufus meant more to the Friends than you can possibly imagine."

I wondered if Oliver Scott had any inkling of what Pop was up to. But he hadn't mentioned him in his letter.

Scott took a sip from his tea. "And we receive some grant support," he continued. "All in all we've managed to keep going."

We'd reached the dining hall. It was open and airy. There were three long wood tables with high-backed chairs and a granite-faced fireplace at one end of the room. A buffet table was nearby, just to the left of the kitchen door. The room was paneled in light, honey-colored birch which added to its warmth.

"We all take turns in the kitchen," Scott said, handing me a tray and silverware. "Someone else cooked this morning so I could work in the shop. Of course, cooking is a craft, too. When a meal is prepared with care, you can taste the joy."

I filled a clay mug with steaming pea soup, and then made a salad of fresh-picked spinach greens, carrots and broccoli. Adding a slab of oven-warm rye bread to my tray, I followed Scott to a table. Several Friends were already there, digging into their lunch: Sarah Bell, who told me she spun wool; Rick Chilson and Nicholas Folts, both of whom worked in the wood shop; and Gary Michaels, a glass blower.

The pea soup was thick with chunks of carrots and a hint of sage.

"Your grandfather was teaching me to fly fish," Folts said, dipping a chunk of bread into his soup. "I surely do miss him."

Sarah Bell handed me the pepper grinder. She was a large, moon-faced woman with chocolate-brown eyes and short-cropped black hair salted with gray. I asked what brought her to Lost Pond. She smiled. Like the others, she seemed eager to tell her story.

"The wood and the flowers, the clay and the sand, the natural materials that we all work with are reservoirs of earth's energy," she began. "As craftspeople, we release this energy and rearrange it in new, more functional forms. In the process, we rearrange ourselves as well," she concluded, her voice softening, her gaze dropping toward the floor.

I thought I followed her logic, but I wasn't sure.

"All of us came here seeking some kind of personal realignment," Chilson added. He was a broad-shouldered man with a clean-shaven, melon-shaped head and wide black eyes that danced in his cherubic face. A stone earring shaped in the form of a cross dangled from his left lobe.

"We were all running from something when we came here…drugs or alcohol, bad marriages or relationships gone sour, jobs with no meaning or little satisfaction," Michaels said.

He looked around the table. There were several nods.

"I survived a car crash that killed two of my best friends. I learned in a flash how fleeting life can be. So I told my boss to shove it, as the song says, and came here to live and pursue my art." He took a bite of his bread. "The Friends, this place, has meant so much to me."

Molly Hunter joined us at the table.

"It's an honor to work with natural materials," Michaels continued. "We feel a reverence for the resources that our Creator shares with us."

"Lost Pond is a magical place that just couldn't be duplicated anywhere else," Hunter added. "When I throw a pot…"

"That means when she forms her work on the potter's wheel," Scott quickly added. That drew a laugh from everyone. I was glad he'd clued me in.

"When I work the clay," she continued, "it comes alive. There is a quality, a uniqueness to work done by hand that cannot be duplicated on a machine. No two pieces are ever quite alike. Like music, you know when a customer is touched by our work. You can see it in their eyes."

"We support each other, encourage each other, and learn from one another," said Bell. "Our work is better because we are one."

"Living and working here in the Adirondacks, in Lost Pond, isolated a bit from the everyday world, we sense the rhythm, the pulse of nature's calendar," Scott added. "Sure, we could make the same pots, tables and chairs somewhere else. But like Molly said, the raw materials would not be the same, the feeling...the energy that goes into each piece wouldn't be the same. The work would be not be the same."

"How 'bout dessert?" Hunter asked. "I made the apple pie myself."

As she started to leave the table, the panes in the windows behind us began to clatter as if a gale has suddenly swept in off the lake.

Womp...womp...womp.

"Simeon Leache," Scott muttered.

We stopped eating and watched the helicopter descend toward the meadow like some monster-sized locust. I wolfed down my last chunk of rye. Scott and I headed for the door. The others remained at the table, their faces staring blankly into their soups and salads. The air was thick with dust, the roar of the motor deafening. We watched the helicopter settle slowly into the high grass. The motor was shut down, but the immense blades continued to spin, albeit ever more slowly. I could see the pilot clearly. His blond hair was cut high and tight, military style. He peered at us momentarily over the top of his sunglasses. After flipping a few switches and peeling off his headphones, he left the cockpit. A moment later, the side door opened, a stairway was lowered, and the pilot walked down the steps. He wore black trousers and a black turtleneck sweater. He was wearing a sidearm. He glared at us once

70

more, than extended his hand to a tall, slender, white-haired woman who made her way cautiously down the steps.

"That's Winnie Stephenson," Scott said through the corner of his mouth. "This has got to be killing her."

A pencil-thin, partially bald man in a charcoal, pin-striped suit clutching a brushed-aluminum briefcase to his miniscule chest was next to make his way down the steps.

"The accountant," I told Scott.

And then Simeon Leache appeared in the doorway. He was a bull-necked, swag-bellied man. His paunch quivered like Jell-O over a turquoise and silver belt buckle the size of a coffee saucer. The helicopter listed toward him as he made his way down the stairway. His skin was liverish and limp, hanging from his sagging jowls like dollops of soft lard. His eyebrows were gray but his hair was brownish orange. Whoever was coloring his hair was doing a lousy job. He was a comical character, but for his eyes. They were small, black and cold and rolled back into his head like the eyes of a great white shark. He was already drenched in sweat as he ambled toward the golf cart that Winnie Stephenson had made sure was waiting for him. She seemed to be pointing something out to him. Then Leache, with his accountant at the wheel, drove off toward Mohawk Lodge. The pilot remained almost at attention by the helicopter's stairway. Was he afraid we'd take it for a hop?

"I want to say hello to Winnie," Scott said. "I'll introduce you." We walked across the meadow to join her.

Winnie Stephenson was a regal woman. Her gray pantsuit was perfectly cut to fit her slender frame. She was small boned, trim and lean, perhaps 60 years old. She walked smartly toward us, but her hazel eyes were tired.

"Oliver, so good to see you,' she said, extending her hand. "I wish I were here under more favorable circumstances."

Scott introduced me.

"I knew your grandfather," she began. "He was a fine man. We spoke just a few weeks ago. Please accept my heartfelt condolences," she added, turning to Scott. "I'm so sorry it's come to this." She waved toward the golf cart that was almost out of sight. "The Friends, their wonderful work, and Lost Pond have always meant a great deal to me, and to the college. But our board's decision is final. The proceeds from the sale here are desperately needed to…well, you don't need to listen to my problems. Mr. Leache is preparing an offer…I'm sorry."

Scott touched her shoulder. "I know you tried."

"Your grandfather said there might be another way, that he needed a few months to put something together, but he never told me what," she said. "Mr. Flynn, do you have any idea what your grandfather might have been thinking about?"

Scott looked at me; this was news to him. How could I tell them what I knew? The truth was I didn't have a clue what Pop had dumped in my lap. I was thinking about just heading back to New York. Sorry, Pop. My chances of tracking down Ethan LaMont, the Last Hermit of the Adirondacks, let alone ever finding von Koenig's diamonds were next to zero, nada, not going to happen. I didn't want to lie, but how could I offer them any hope that Lost Pond could be saved from Simeon Leache? I needed more time.

"My grandfather had done quite a bit of research on a novel," I began. "I've read some of what he'd learned, particularly about the history of this area, but I don't know if any of it will be helpful in solving the problem all of you are facing."

That was as truthful as I could be.

"Your grandfather asked the college to delay acceptance of any offer until April next year," Stephenson continued. "He also wanted the college's assurances that if another potential buyer were to match Leache's offer—and that buyer would ensure the preservation of Lost Pond and the Friends' lease—than that would be the offer accepted by the college. The board approved both these stipulations the day after your grandfather died."

"What's Leache's timetable? Has he submitted a formal offer yet?" I asked.

"The man with him, that's Chester Mann, his chief financial officer," Stephenson began. "They're looking at our structures, what they may continue to use, and what they'll simply plow under or burn to the ground. Leache has not submitted his offer, but unofficially he's told me it will be ten million dollars, which is a million more than our asking price. He's confident that no one will top him."

"What about the state?" I asked. "Haven't they bought up nearly a million acres over the last eight or ten years?"

"They have," Stephenson replied, "but New York State is billions in debt. And Simeon Leache has friends in high places. No one at the state level is going to try to stop him."

"So that gives us, what, about six months?" Scott asked. "What in the world was your grandfather was up to?"

I shrugged my shoulders. I don't think Scott quite believed me.

"I told Leache and his accountant that I would meet them at the lodge," Stephenson said. "You might as well meet him, Mr. Flynn."

Oliver Scott excused himself. "I've got to get back to work."

"If your grandfather was on to anything that will prevent this..." Stephenson said as we walked across the meadow. "Is there anything you want to tell me that perhaps you didn't want to discuss in front of Oliver Scott?"

Winnie Stephenson was a very perceptive woman. She was reading my eyes like she'd known me all my life.

"Let's walk down by the lake," I suggested. "There ARE some things you need to know."

Chapter Seven

Simeon Leache didn't bother to get up from his chair. Shaking his hand was like squeezing a warm, wet sponge.

"Flynn...Flynn?" Leache asked, his eyes darting around the room as if he expected to find what he was looking for written on the walls. "Rufus Flynn, that's it. He sent me a letter, rather threatening, I recall. I've asked my attorney to look into the threats he made against our project here," Leache continued. "Who is Rufus Flynn to you?"

"He was my grandfather," I said. "He's dead."

"Well, I suppose your loss is my gain," Leache replied. "Of course I am sorry for your loss," he added as a meaningless afterthought. "But your grandfather's opposition to the development of the Institute here...to the Great Awakening...it was dead on arrival."

Leache cast a quick glance at the accountant, Chester Mann, who returned a weasel-like smile.

"The Great Awakening?" I asked.

"America must return to its righteous roots, Mr. Flynn. I founded the Institute for the Preservation of American Values for the purpose of reviving our Christian ideals, the very principals upon which our great country was founded." Leache's chest swelled with every word, his face reddening like a ripe tomato. "We will cleanse our schools of teachers who edify perversion instead of patriotism. We will drive from our shores the alien hordes that are undermining our culture, these immigrants who don't even want to speak our language, who are turning our great cities into Third World ghettos."

Until coming face-to-face with Simeon Leache I'd simply

written him off as just another media buffoon. He wasn't making me laugh now.

"America is a nation of immigrants," I countered. "You could make a strong case that our diversity of culture strengthens the whole idea of America...'give me your tired, your poor, your huddled masses yearning to breathe free.' Maybe you should take a ride out to the Statue of Liberty and read it for yourself," I added.

"It was a gift from the French," Leache sneered.

Winnie Stephenson walked into the room with Cyrus Black. He was carrying several thick manila folders.

"Our republic is in peril," Leache continued. "There are enemies within, determined to create a North American trading colossus, a virtual union of Mexico, Canada and the United States. That will be the end of America as we know it."

"I have those numbers you wanted to look at," Black said, reluctantly handing the folders to the accountant.

I welcomed his timely interruption. Leache hauled himself from the chair and shuffled across the room toward Chester Mann. "If you'll excuse me, Mr. Flynn, I have to look over the lodge's books. Perhaps we can continue this debate another time."

Debate, I thought, *you pompous bigoted bastard.*

Winnie Stephenson motioned for me to join her on the porch. We found two comfortable wicker chairs in a quiet corner with a breathtaking view of the lake.

"Your grandfather called Leache a counterfeit patriot," Stephenson said.

"After what I just heard, I'd say that was putting it mildly," I replied.

"Leache's aim is to create a new generation of journalists, teachers and clergy, and most importantly, political candidates, who will espouse what is, in fact, a white supremacist agenda."

"But why establish his so-called institute here?" I asked.

"He needs to sell his movement as a spiritual one," Stephenson replied. "He recruits many of his followers from radical religious movements. By locating in a wilderness setting, in the heart of the Adirondack Park, he'll create the illusion of a monastery, void of distractions, where his recruits can focus totally on their mission."

"So we have about six months to find another buyer, one who will preserve the historic character of Lost Pond, perhaps even enhance it, and provide for the continuation of the Friends work. Is that about right?" I asked.

"That's correct," Stephenson replied. "Leache will submit his formal offer next week. But as I mentioned, the college retains the right to accept a matching offer if it includes the preservation of Lost Pond."

She looked wistfully out over the lake.

"The odds have to be one in a million, but will you try to help us?"

■   ■   ■

Winnie Stephenson, looking like a prisoner, had peered sorrowfully out the side window of the Leache's helicopter as it lifted off. I'd walked back to Pop's cabin and re-read everything he'd left behind. Now I needed to talk to Doc Ingram or Megan Seagar, whomever I found first.

Doc was easy. It was just past five. His gin was freshly poured.

"Have a martini," he said, peering over the half eyeglasses that rested near the tip of his pink whiskey nose.

"I'll skip the pepper-stuffed olives tonight," I replied.

Sandy nodded and went to work mixing my drink.

"So?" Doc asked, lifting his glass and taking a long sip.

"So what?" I countered, but knowing exactly where he was going.

"Your grandfather's treasure hunt." Doc was grinning ear-to-ear.

"Mission impossible," I countered.

Sandy handed me my martini. I dove into it. The gin seared down my throat like a prairie fire.

"Straight up, Doc," I continued. "Do you and Megan believe what my grandfather dug up is true? Or were you both just humoring him, before he died?"

Doc took another generous sip from his drink. "I think Rufus nailed it."

He speared an olive from his martini and rolled it around in his mouth, savoring its gin-soaked sweetness.

"Should be one hell of an adventure," he added with a wink. "Wish I was going with you."

"If I'm going anywhere I'm going back to New York City," I replied. I don't think Doc believed me. And I wasn't so sure myself anymore. "You and Megan are the only people who knew what my grandfather was up to, right?" I asked.

"That's the way Rufus wanted it," Doc replied. "That's the way it's got to be. This could involve one hell of a lot of money, you know."

"Is there anyone else we can trust?" I continued. "I wouldn't have a clue where to begin looking for Ethan LaMont. I'd need Stoner for that."

"Stoner will keep his mouth shut, and you don't have to tell him everything," Doc replied.

"Simeon Leache was here today, but I suppose you know that," I said.

"Heard the chopper coming in and I headed in the opposite direction," Doc replied. "Leache has been here before, checking the place out. Did he see Cyrus Black?"

"Yeah, he was at the lodge, looking at Black's financials. Why?"

"I don't think Leache will tear the lodge down," Doc replied. "He'll keep it for VIP guests, big contributors. My guess is that Cyrus Black will run it for him. So be careful. If Black gets wind of what we're up to, Leache could know about it in a heartbeat."

Sandy headed for the door. "I'm goin' out for a smoke. Help yourself."

Doc raised a bushy eyebrow. "Don't mind if I do. Join me?" he asked.

I drained my drink and slid Doc my empty glass. He slipped behind the bar. A man and woman walked in. Seeing no one to seat them, they took a table by the window. Both appeared in their late sixties or early seventies. They were wearing identical Barbour jackets the color of ripe avocados, brown corduroy pants and knee-high green rubber boots. They could have just stepped from the tweedy pages of an Orvis catalog.

Hakeem dashed from the kitchen carrying two glasses of water and menus.

"*Messieurs*," he said with a smile, and then rushed to welcome his arriving guests.

Arlo Stoner slid through the kitchen door just as it was swinging closed.

"Guided them today," he mumbled. He was chewing on the crusty heel of a loaf of Hakeem's bread.

"We got some nice brook trout, one a three-pounder." He grabbed a bottle of Saranac from the cooler.

"How was your tip?" Doc asked as he handed me my fresh drink.

Stoner flashed Doc a wide grin. "I do love these sports

from the big city!" Then he looked at me. "Wanna go fishing?"

I took a quick sip from my drink. "Wanna find the Last Hermit of the Adirondacks?"

Stoner erupted in laughter. "Know what they say about martinis, Flynn?"

"No, what do they say about martinis?" I asked.

Stoner took a swig from his beer.

"Martinis are like breasts on a woman."

He paused momentarily for effect.

"One's not enough, but three are too many." He polished off his beer with one long swallow, and then grabbed another.

"Why did Rufus want to find the Hermit, who we now know is one Ethan LaMont?" Stoner asked.

Doc shot me a look of surprise.

"What makes you think Rufus has something to do with this?" he asked.

Stone took a swig from his beer.

"Rufus asked me if I'd ever seen him. I said no. Asked me if I thought I could find him. Why? I asked. Man wants to be alone. You gotta respect that. And I don't want the law using me to collar him. Hell, LaMont's a kind of hero around here, I said. Breaks into some rich guy's camp and they just about put up a sign—the Last Hermit slept here! Well, old Rufus got serious. Said if it was really important, could I do it."

"Well?" Doc asked. "What did you tell him?"

"Maybe…maybe not."

Doc and I waited. Stoner had more to say.

He drained half his beer in a three fast swallows.

"The Hermit will have to find *you*," Stoner said. He was looking at me.

"What do you mean…find ME?" I asked.

Stoner paused to wave to the couple he'd guided that

afternoon. "This Last Hermit stuff, it was pretty damn important to your grandfather," he began. "He didn't tell me why, and I didn't ask. But he did tell me one thing."

"What was that?" Doc asked.

"That the city slicker here would finish what he'd started," Stoner said, pointing the neck of his beer bottle at my nose. "It won't be easy. Troopers, DEC police have been after him for years. If they can't find him with helicopters and dogs...but one man might have a chance...a man without a gun."

"How do we know he's anywhere near here?" I asked. "This is nuts."

"We don't," Stoner began. "But if he isn't, he's probably movin' this way. Winter's coming on. He's got a nice choice of camps east and north of here. My guess is he's scoutin' 'em now, waitin' for the first good snow to close the seasonal roads. Then he'll be fartin' in silk," Stoner added.

"So where do you think he MIGHT be—what's your best guess?" Doc asked.

Stoner looked at me, then at Doc. "You boys ARE serious about this?"

"Very serious," Doc replied.

Arlo Stoner paused to drain his beer.

"I'd wager he's on the Hogback—or heading that way. From there he can slip down to Little Buck Lake and have his choice of some prime Algonquin Club real estate. Or...he could be on the Otter River, out of sight but just a day's paddle to either Snowshoe Lake or the Osprey Chain."

Doc bit into his last olive.

"So you'll help us?"

Stoner pulled at his chin whiskers, and then he smiled. "Got a couple of days open."

I knew then I was hooked for good.

MARK W. HOLDREN

Chapter Eight

The woodpecker was back at it outside Pop's bedroom window, pounding away at the bug-infested tree like a boxer working on a light bag. Who needed an alarm clock? My head was splitting, again. A second night of slamming martinis with Doc Ingram had just about finished me off. Megan had stopped by while Doc and I were eating dinner. She asked me again about taking a paddle in the morning. Stoner and I wouldn't be leaving until the following day, so I'd jumped at the chance. I thought a little tune-up with Megan would help me get ready for several days in the backcountry with Arlo Stoner. It was just past six. Megan had said to meet her at the dock at seven-thirty. I eased my way out of bed and stumbled toward the coffee maker. I had an hour and a half to get my act together.

■   ■   ■

My head was beginning to clear. Three cups of black coffee and the icy morning air were bringing me back to life. There'd been a heavy frost. The leaves were pouring down from the trees as if someone were dumping them by the barrelful. The scent of wood smoke drifted through the woods, invisible to the eye, but captivating to the nose.

The kayaks were resting in the black, mirror-still water like submarines; only the conning towers were missing. A cold yet steam-like fog was just beginning to lift from warmer surface of the lake.

Megan tossed me a life jacket. "Right on time. Put this on. Hate to lose you now."

I zipped up. She handed me a paddle.

"This stuff's already burning off," she said, waving a hand out toward the lake. She untied the kayaks from the dock and pulled them onto the beach.

"It's easier to get in these things from shore, especially if you aren't used to crawling in and out of one, which I don't think you are," she added with a knowing smile.

"Thanks for your concern." I added.

She wiped both seats dry with a towel, then opened the hatch in what I assumed was her boat and stuffed a backpack into the hold.

"Lunch...I put a water bottle in your boat. Kayaked before?"

"Not in a while," I replied, easing myself into the cockpit like a race driver sliding into a car at the Indy 500. I turned the paddle in my hands, getting the feel of it, and then I pushed off into the water. Megan slipped into her boat and we paddled into the mist. The kayaks sliced through the glassy water like well-honed carving knives. I took a long, deep breath, then another. I was beginning to wonder why I'd kept myself from the mountains for so long. Passing round the point, a loon popped from beneath the water not ten yards off my bow. Cocking its head, it cast us a wary eye. Then, deciding we weren't a threat, it cruised along with us for a minute or two before diving back below the surface.

"We'll just hug the shore for awhile," Megan said as she pulled alongside. "I love the smell of the leaves in the fall, kind of like caramel and maple syrup."

We drifted quietly, drinking in the moment.

"Not like the streets of Manhattan," I added finally.

"And what do the streets of Manhattan smell like?" Megan asked.

"Red onion relish and frying peppers," I replied. "God I

do miss it so."

"I hope you're kidding," she replied.

"Well, I could get used to this in a real hurry," I added. "I was just thinking about how much I've missed all this. It's been a long time."

An otter slid down a steep mud bank and disappeared into the amber water.

"Hey, did you see that?" I cried out.

"We introduced a pair of otters here last year," Megan replied. "They appear to be doing fine."

We held fast to the shoreline, maneuvering a couple of times around the tops of several massive boulders that rose from of the water like mountain peaks. The mist had pretty much burned off the water. I could see the far shore of the lake now, a sun-splashed palette of oranges, reds and yellows.

"Where are we headed?" I asked.

"North Bay. We'll beach the kayaks at the trailhead, and then hike to the overlook. Great spot for an early lunch."

I followed along in Megan's wake. She paddled with a graceful, natural rhythm. Sitting several inches below the lake's surface, a kayak paddler is embraced by the water instead of simply skimming over it as one would in a boat or canoe.

"It's pretty shallow up ahead," she called back over her shoulder. "There's a narrow channel, though. Follow me."

We slid into a thick bed of reeds that rose from the tawny water like the quills of a porcupine. The water was just inches deep. Twice I had to throw my weight forward, urging the kayak off the sandy bottom. Megan, weighing probably sixty pounds less than me, slithered her boat easily through the grassy maze. Just as we cleared the reeds, a noisy gaggle of mergansers splashed off just in front of us. Once airborne, they made a tight turn and flew back out into the lake.

"That's an eagle's nest up there," Megan said, pointing to the top of a towering white pine. The nest, more than a hundred feet off the ground, was made of tree branches—ample enough for a small child to sit in without fear of breaking through.

"I saw one when Stoner brought me in from the Landing," I replied.

North Bay's shoreline was thick with flaming red maples and brilliant white birches, their golden-yellow leaves quaking in the rising breeze. We cruised past a small island, perhaps a couple of acres in size. A stone chimney rose from behind a dense stand of spruce. I wondered whose cabin it might have been, a trapper, perhaps, maybe Louie LaMont? We watched a kingfisher dive from a dead beech limb, hitting the water like a stone. It rose instantly with a small fish wiggling its last in the fisher's beak. Leaving the island behind us, the bay dissolved into a river of grass. We passed easily this time through another thicket of reeds, the floodplain narrowing to a twisting stream choked with cattails and pickerelweed. A blue heron, startled by our presence, lifted gracefully from the shallows, flying upstream and out of sight, only to be rousted by us again when we rounded the next bend. Then a brownish, stocky bird burst from the tall grass.

Kok...kok...kok.

"What is that?" I asked.

"It's a bittern, surprised it hasn't lit out for Florida by now."

"Not a very bright bird," I added.

The water was soon littered with plant stems and leaves.

"What's all this stuff?" I asked.

"Muskrats," Megan replied. "They're storing food for winter. They'll swim up into the pile and chow down, until the coyotes find them," she added.

We flushed the heron once more before landing the kayaks at a dock that had seen better days. Half its planking was gone. It was listing like a sinking ship into an algae-ooze the color and smell of rotting avocado. Megan climbed from her boat into the yellow-green slime. I did the same, though not as gracefully. She tied off our kayaks, pulled on her backpack, and we slogged ashore.

"How far from here?" I asked, reaching for my water bottle.

"An hour and change, mostly flat, until the last half-a-mile," she replied, stoking up on water as well.

The trail cut through a jumble of black ash, balsam fir, and white cedar. We walked for about ten minutes or so, all the while serenaded by a boisterous chickadee flitting around us with its whistled song. Then the trail intersected with an old logging road.

"We hang a right here," she advised.

I followed along, leaving the marshy woods behind. We were climbing steadily now, the trees of the swamp giving way to beech, yellow birch and sugar maple.

"That's an old beaver pond," Megan said, pointing to shallow pond thick with what she told me was leather leaf, sheep laurel and bog rosemary. Nearby a woodpecker hammered away on a dead tamarack. The old road made a couple of turns before crossing the rusting rails of a long-abandoned railroad. Megan stopped and took a long drink of water. I followed her cue. She tossed me a sandwich-size plastic bag.

"Walnuts and raisins?" she asked.

I took a handful and poured them into my mouth.

"Are these the same tracks that cross the Otter River, wherever that is from here?" I asked.

"You must be thinking about Louie LaMont. The Otter's

just below Lost Pond, about six miles south of here," she replied.

I took another drink.

"Let's talk about LaMont over lunch," I suggested.

She tucked away her water bottle. "Follow me."

I tried "tightrope" walking the rails, but quickly found that wasn't a way to make much progress. And hopping from one creosote soaked tie to another wasn't much fun either. The stone railbed, despite its banking, provided the best footing.

We'd walked only a few hundred yards when a small flatcar chugged around the bend just in front of us.

"What in hell is that?" I asked.

"Hunters," Megan replied. "Deer season starts in a few weeks. They use the tracks to get to their camps."

The homemade contraption sputtered past us. It was powered by what looked like a garden tractor motor. Three heavyset men were seated on a stack of boxes and folded white tarps. One toasted me with his can of Budweiser. A red-faced man sitting on a trunk-sized cooler raised his rifle into the air. The third man beer tossed his empty Bud can back at me as they passed.

"The last of the red-blooded American sportsmen," I muttered.

"A lot of hunters use the old rail line this way," Megan replied. "They get to drinking at night, racing up and down the tracks. Every once in a while one of them gets himself killed."

■　　■　　■

We reached the overview thirty minutes later. The trail broke from the trees onto slabs of sun-splashed granite. The view was stunning, encompassing most of Lake Mohawk glittering below like a blanket of shimmering jewels. The distant High Peaks rolled over the eastern horizon in lazy ribbons of moonstone blue. Megan dropped her pack and, using it as a pillow, kicked back on the warm rock ledge.

"This was your grandfather's favorite spot. He called it his sacred place," she said.

I sat down beside her. A raven swung by just over our heads. It would no doubt return for any crumbs we might leave behind. A pair of black-capped chickadees had the same idea. They took up their vigil on a nearby spruce limb, hopeful they could snare a snack before the raven drove them off.

"Rufus didn't wear his faith on his sleeve," she continued. "But he was one of the most spiritual people I knew. He told me he didn't know if there was a God, but in these mountains, at this overlook in particular, he said he could feel a presence, a power that overwhelmed him."

She rolled slightly toward me on her elbow. "This is the first time I've been up here since he died."

"What was my grandfather like...the last hours of his life? What did he talk about?" I asked.

"He was incredibly serene, comforted that he was dying on his own terms," she began. "Rufus talked about his incredibly full life...that he'd been blessed with good health, until the end. He regretted the collapse of his marriage, after what, nearly fifty years? He still loved your grandmother. But he recognized they'd become very different people. He was also very proud of you. He was sorry that you and he had drifted apart, but he understood that was just part of his getting old. 'Life moves on,' he said."

"Selfishness, pure and simple," I added. "I was too busy making money."

We watched an osprey rise and fall with the currents over the lake. I wished I'd shared this place with Pop just once before he died.

"Your grandfather said the last years of his life, his time here at Lost Pond, were the happiest of his life. He was privileged, he said, to have experienced the magic of these mountains, before the magic is gone forever."

"What do you mean, gone?" I asked. "The Adirondack Park is a park, I mean it's protected, forever wild, isn't it?"

"Protected? Excuse me," she began. "Hundreds of our lakes and ponds are devoid of fish, due to acid rain. Mercury poisoning could very well kill off our loon population. Now climate changes are coming. Warmer temperatures will wipe out our hardwood trees. In just a century, or less, this will be pretty much a soft pine forest, like Georgia looks today. Snow will fall only on the highest peaks. The lakes will be ice-free. But that's just the tip of the melting iceberg, so to speak. A culture, a way of life, is disappearing as well."

"What are you talking about?" I asked. "Things up here look pretty much the way I remember them."

"Land values are ten times what they were just twenty years ago," she replied. "Middle-class people, working people, are finding it increasingly difficult to live here. You're either very rich, able to afford a million-dollar vacation home, or you're in the service class, tending to the needs of the wealthy. Young people are moving out. They can't afford to buy a home. School districts are merging, just to survive."

"Pretty depressing," I said. "I had no idea."

"That's why preserving places like Lost Pond are so important," she replied. "You asked what your grandfather was talking about, in the days before he died. He hoped you'd finish what he'd started."

Megan Seagar was crying now.

I took my handkerchief and wiped the tears from her cheeks. She sniffled, and then tried to smile.

"Let's have our lunch."

She opened her pack and handed me a sandwich wrapped in aluminum foil and a fresh bottle of water.

"I hope you like turkey. The bread's homemade, and so is the mustard."

We dug into our lunch while the drifting clouds cast ever shifting shadows over the water below. Each of us was lost for the moment in our own thoughts. We finished our sandwiches. She tossed me an apple and bit into her own.

"So what do you think?" she asked at last.

"Great apple," I replied.

"That's not what I was asking. What do you think about your grandfather's plan, about saving Lost Pond?"

I took another bite of my apple.

"I'm leaving in the morning...with Arlo Stoner. Ethan LaMont is out there...somewhere."

She threw her arms around me.

"I knew you'd do it!" She kissed me warmly on my cheek. "Your grandfather was right about you."

"If I had any doubts...you closed the deal, up here."

I hugged her back, kissing her lightly on the lips. She lingered for a just a moment and then pulled away.

"So who is Megan Seagar?" I asked. "You know about me, about my grandfather. What's a nice girl like you doing in a place like this?" I added with a laugh.

She tossed her apple core back into the woods. "The mice will love it." Then she took a long drink of water. "I was pretty idealistic when I graduated from college," she began. "You know the speech, 'you can change the world.' So I went into teaching. I told you about the discipline problems, the physical threats. Sometimes I felt like a lion tamer at the circus. The only thing missing was the whip and chair. But you can't blame the kids, not totally. Their parents are both working, but the family is still in debt up to its eyeballs. These kids aren't stupid. They see the future. It's not pretty."

"So you just chucked it?" I asked.

"There was more to it than that." She took another drink of water. "I was engaged, would have been married by now, probably have started a family. Todd and I bought a house. Life was good. Then one afternoon he hopped on his bike and never came back. A drunk driver hit him. He was killed instantly."

I put my arm around her. "I'm sorry." Her head dropped onto my shoulder.

"That was three years ago," she continued. "I needed to start over, so I came up here."

"Any thoughts on what you might do, long term?" I asked.

"Well, I guess that depends on you."

"Me? We just met," I joked.

She laughed. "I meant it depends on whether or not you find Ethan LaMont, the diamonds, and what happens to all this," she added, sweeping her hand out over lake. "I'd like to grow my business in Lost Pond, support the Friends, and see if I can become a decent artist."

"I'd say you're already there," I said.

"I've got a long way to go. Your grandfather wanted me to focus more on my art and forget the store," she said.

"I think he's given you a little nudge in that direction."

"What do you mean?" she asked.

"He's left you a hundred thousand dollars in his will."

"No," she stammered. "Your grandfather said he'd help me, even if it killed him." She smiled, but tears were running from her eyes. She looked away for a moment, and then rubbed her tears away with a shirtsleeve.

"Rufus told me you weren't married."

"I was engaged, to my boss's daughter. Mega mistake.

When I was fired, she fired me."

"Sounds like it wouldn't have lasted very long," she said.

"We Flynns haven't been lucky in love."

She raised an eyebrow.

"My parents divorced when I was in high school. Grandfather divorced, finally."

"Maybe your luck will change," she added with a warm smile. "Going back to Wall Street when this is over?"

I kissed her lightly on the forehead. "That depends on you."

She laughed. "I guess I asked for that."

We hung out at the overlook until mid-afternoon, watching the clouds roll across the cobalt sky like covered wagons crossing the Great Plains. The stillness was broken only by an occasional scolding from the raven. Its patience with us was wearing thin.

■　　■　　■

We paddled back to Lost Pond pretty much in silence. A brisk west wind was whipping the lake into a brisk chop; keeping as dry as possible required all of our attention. We were back at the dock just past four. I offered to buy Megan dinner, my way of saying thanks for a great day...a day I didn't want to end. She asked for a rain check, but warmly, I thought. She had to pack several paintings for shipment to Philadelphia in the morning. So I headed back to Pop's cabin for a hot shower and some dry clothes.

■　　■　　■

Doc Ingram was perched at the bar. "How'd it go...at the overlook?"

How did he know I was there? Did this guy miss

anything?

"Megan told me she was taking you on a little tour," Doc added. "What do you think?"

"About the view?" I replied, knowing that's not where he was headed.

Doc smiled. "Have a martini."

"I'll skip the see-throughs tonight," I replied. "Where's Sandy?"

Doc shrugged. "Smokes too much."

I helped myself to one of Pop's Red Eyes.

"I don't know which I like better, the booze or the fruit," Doc said, fishing the last olive from his martini. "Megan's a fine woman, fine indeed. Old Rufus said if he was forty years younger…"

Hakeem burst through the kitchen door.

"*Messieurs!* Tonight you must try my scallops with anise sauce!"

How could we refuse?

■　　■　　■

It was just past nine when I got back to the cabin. I started a fire, settled into Pop's chair, and lit up a Hoyo de Monterrey. Savoring a long delicious puff, then another, I wondered what in hell I'd gotten myself into. I was coming up for just two or three days, wrapping up Pop's affairs, and getting back to my poker game. Now, just after daybreak, I'd be tramping into the backcountry in search of a ghost. I took another long pull on the cigar. The smoke curled up toward the ceiling like a curious serpent. I'd been in Lost Pond what, forty-eight hours, and already the place was growing on me. I was beginning to see why Pop had found this quirky outpost so irresistible. The Cuban cigar was now drawing as cleanly as the fireplace. I threw on my fleece and walked out on the deck. The stars glittered like...well...diamonds in the ink-black sky. I smiled; maybe that's where Louis LaMont stashed von Koenig's long-lost gems. No wonder no one had found them. A coyote welcomed the night with a long, mournful wail. The wind was still, yet I trembled in the black cold that was descending over the lake. The trees were mostly bare. The first snows of winter could come any day. But the process of renewal was already under way. The seeds of spring had already been sown.

Chapter Nine

"Hello."

It was Megan. She was knocking softly on the screen door. Her voice warmed the cold cabin, the fire having sputtered out while I'd slept.

"Come on in," I shouted.

She found me sorting through Pop's camping gear. Everything I could find—tent, tarps, sleeping bag, self-inflating air mattress, cook kit, plastic water bottles, packs, assorted straps, bungee cords, and rope—I'd spread out on the living room floor. I hadn't come to Lost Pond equipped to live in the woods for a single night let alone a week or more.

"Thought you might like to take some of these fresh-baked muffins along," she said. I could smell their cinnamon sweetness wafting through the paper bag she handed me.

"Thanks, why wait? I just put on a fresh pot of coffee."

She tossed back her hair, making me wish I was heading for the woods with her instead of Arlo Stoner. We poured our coffee and walked out onto the deck. There was a hint of wood smoke on the icy morning air. Gazing over the shimmering water, inhaling the moment, we receded into our own thoughts. She tossed her hair again. Our eyes met.

"Kind of wish you were coming along," I blurted out.

She smiled and took a sip of coffee.

"I'll help you get packed."

■　　■　　■

We could hear Stoner coming, his truck coughing and wheezing down the driveway. He left it running, just in case, I imagined, that it might expire at last.

"Top of the morning, Flynn," he crowed.

Two small canoes were roped to the truck bed. There were also a couple of orange waterproof bags. I tossed in my gear.

"I see The Major's still kickin'," Megan said.

Stoner patted a rusted fender. "The Major's amazin'."

"So where are we headed, I mean, with the truck? I didn't think there were any roads?" I asked.

"The Ten Dollar Road, only road we got," Stoner replied.

"It's an old logging road," Megan added. "It leads down to the Otter River. You're in for a treat."

"Climb in," Stoner said. "Kiss him goodbye, Megan, you may never see him again!"

She blew me a kiss. I wished it were more.

Stoner yanked his truck into reverse and we sputtered back up the driveway. He spun the wheel and, jamming The Major into first gear, we lurched down the road, past the lodge and over the railroad tracks. There, Stoner made a sharp left-hand turn onto a dirt road I hadn't noticed before.

"Welcome to the Ten Dollar Road," he announced.

"Do they call it that because that's all it cost to build?" I shouted over the noise of the motor.

"Nah," Stoner yelled back. "In the old days the loggers came upriver and took the road to Lost Pond. The sporting gals at the Tall Timber charged the boys ten dollars for their favors."

"The Tall Timber?" I asked. "Where's that?"

"It ain't," Stoner replied. "It burned to the ground in the nineteen-thirties. All the boys could save was the foundation," he added with a laugh.

The Major was gaining speed. Stoner shifted into second, then third. We careened down a long hill. The truck shook like a shaggy wet dog. I looked for something to hold on to but there was nothing that didn't feel as if it was about to fall off.

"Cigar?" Stoner shouted, pulling a thick black stogie from his shirt pocket.

"No thanks," I replied. I could barely breathe. The cab was filled with gut-wrenching smoke. It was pouring up from The Major's broken tailpipe, which I could see through a gaping hole in the floor under my feet.

Stoner lit his cigar with a battered metal pocket lighter. "Adventure, Flynn. Always light a cigar on the start of a new adventure."

"That a Zippo?" I asked. "Don't see many anymore."

"Belonged to my father," Stoner replied. "He carried it across Europe with Patton's Third Army."

He handed me the lighter. "See that dent? German sniper. The Zippo kept the bullet out of my old man's heart. He just died a couple of years ago."

At the bottom of the hill we splashed across a small stream. It twisted like ribbon candy through a wide meadow of gnawed tree stumps, wild grasses and aspen saplings.

"Beavers will be back in two, maybe three years," Stoner muttered through the corner of his mouth. "We'll have a hell of time crossing here then."

He downshifted into second gear. The truck ground its way up and over the ridge. Then we plunged down the other side, crossing another small feeder stream before reaching the end of the road.

"Here she is, the Otter River...just rollin' along," Stoner crooned.

He yanked The Major into a grassy clearing and turned off the motor. It spit and stammered, backfired once, then died, this time perhaps forever.

The river was the color of dark tea.

Woo-e-e-e-ek...woo-e-e-e-ek.

It was a hen wood duck. She jumped off the water and peeled upstream.

We pulled the canoes from the truck.

"I can't believe how light this is," I said. "What's it weigh, fifteen pounds maybe?"

"That's about right," Stoner replied. "They're Kevlar."

The canoes were amber-colored. You sat in them like a kayak, rather than on a raised seat, like a standard canoe. Stoner tossed me a kayak-like paddle. The shaft was made of ash. Its Kevlar blades were feathered to reduce wind resistance.

"Let me take a look at your gear," Stoner said, as he began sorting through my duffle. "We'll be traveling fast and light, so there's no sense dragging stuff along we don't need. I've got you pretty much covered, anyway."

He stuffed my rain gear, extra clothes and toilet kit into one of the waterproof bags.

"This one's yours. Don't lose it," he added.

We stowed our gear in the canoes and pushed off into the Otter River.

Stoner was enjoying the remnants of his cigar. We drifted slowly in the current, dipping our paddles only occasionally to keep on course. The river took a series of meandering turns through an ever-widening wetland choked with speckled alders, dogwoods and mountain holly.

"So what's the plan?" I asked.

Stoner took a long drag on his cigar.

"We're heading northeast," he began. "There's about five miles of river between us and Snowshoe Lake." He took another puff from his cigar. "Look around, what do you see?"

"Looks like we're in the middle of a swamp," I replied.

"Precisely," Stoner replied. "Not a lot of high ground. But

there are a couple of feeder streams, Rocky Brook and Half Moon Creek. LaMont could reach high ground from either. We'll take a look."

The sweet aroma of Stoner's cigar was growing on me; I should have grabbed one when I had the chance. It wasn't a Cuban but it was good enough for a river paddle. I was glad I'd brought along a few of Pop's Montecristos for the campfire.

"So what would Ethan LaMont do...when he got to higher ground?" I asked.

"He'd skedaddle back into the bush, covering his tracks as he went. He'd most likely build three, maybe four shanty camps, and move from one to the next every few days.

"What's a shanty camp?" I asked.

"Nothing more than tree branches over a crossbar, covered with more branches, then chunks of bark and leaves."

"Sounds like we'd have better luck finding Elvis," I added.

"If Elvis hasn't left the building, we should find some sign," Stoner said.

"The rest will be up to you."

■　　■　　■

We reached the mouth of Rocky Brook about an hour later. It wasn't much wider than my canoe. I followed Stoner as he paddled through a jungle of cattails and pickerelweed. Three times we had to climb from the boats and wade through shin-deep mud.

"Been a dry summer," Stoner mumbled. "Crick's about dried up."

It took us half an hour to clear the marsh. We pulled our boats up under a stand of hemlock and cedar. Stoner walked slowly along the shore, occasionally running his hand over the grass on the bank.

"One thing's for sure," he said.

"What's that?"

"LaMont hasn't been here, at least in the last few days."

"So what do we do, move on?" I asked.

"Because he hasn't been here doesn't mean he isn't up there," Stoner replied, pointing up the steep ridge.

"Where's his boat?" I asked.

Stoner gave me his best evil eye.

"If he is here, his boat is stashed where we'd have to trip over it to find it. Or he took it with him."

"Took it where?" I asked.

"Half Moon Pond," Stoner said, grabbing his pack. I hadn't noticed that his was attached to an aluminum frame which he then attached to his canoe with two wing nuts. Next he bolted an aluminum rod, perhaps three feet long, to the pack. The opposite end he attached with another wing nut to one of the canoe's gunwales. Then, tipping the canoe up and walking under it he pulled on the pack, which now supported the boat, leaving both his hands free.

"Pretty damn clever," I admitted.

"They don't call it a Lost Pond boat for nothing," Stoner replied. He grabbed his paddle that he'd leaned against a hemlock.

"What about my boat?" I asked.

"We'll only need one," Stoner replied. "Half Moon holds some nice brook trout, pure Adirondack strain. You can catch our dinner. Let's go."

We paralleled the stream for several hundred yards before breaking off into a dense stand of white pine. The trail had been pretty much obliterated by blow downs, forcing us to crawl over or under dozens of shattered trees that had been ripped from the earth by their roots.

"Soil here's sandy, root systems are shallow," Stoner said. "Trees don't stand a chance in the Big Wind."

We began climbing the ridge. The steep slope, blanketed with pine needles, was like walking up a mountain of marbles. A couple of times I thought I might slide all the way back to the marsh. But Stoner moved at a steady pace, never breaking stride, never losing his footing. Crossing a sun-splashed clearing, I could see the river winding through the marsh below.

"See why LaMont likes this ground?" Stoner said. "He can spot anyone approaching from either direction."

I was wondering if LaMont was already watching us. Perhaps he'd set a trap to slow us down, one of those snares that would hook my leg and toss me into the air like a rag doll. Or maybe he'd dug a pit.... I'd been in the woods just an hour and already the Last Hermit of the Adirondacks was messing with my mind.

The conifers gave way to a mix of hemlock and hardwoods. One red squirrel, then another, scolded us soundly for tramping through their territory. A black-capped chickadee added its own *fee-bee-ee...fee-bee* to the squirrels' constant chatter.

I was taking a drink from my water bottle when Stoner stopped dead in his tracks.

"Don't move."

I didn't. "What is it?" I whispered, "LaMont?"

"No...*des ours*."

"Des what?" I stammered.

"Bears," Stoner replied. "That's French...two cubs. Mama can't be far away."

Now I could see them. They were just fifteen or twenty yards in front of us. They'd come to a screeching halt as well.

They eyed us with caution and a good dose of curiosity, their heads rocking back and forth like bobble heads. Stoner, standing under his canoe, must have been a strange sight indeed. Then the sow made her presence known with a long, guttural hiss. The cubs got the message, high-tailing it up the nearest pine. Mama then lumbered down the trail directly toward us. Stoner began backing up. I followed his lead.

"Slowly...slowly. Just give her some space," he whispered.

We'd backed down the trail maybe ten or twelve yards. The bear stopped, hissed one more time, then turned and ambled back toward her cubs.

"What now," I whispered, my words barely clearing my bone-dry throat.

"We wait."

Stoner dug out his own water bottle.

"How long?" I asked.

"Long enough," Stoner said. "They'll move off in a few minutes. Here, have a taste of last year's deer...one of them."

He handed me a chunk of venison jerky. I took a bite.

"Let it soften in your mouth," he advised.

"How far to this pond," I mumbled.

"Oh, another half hour or so...depends on how long we're stuck here in traffic," he added with a laugh.

The jerky tasted of sugar and soy sauce. I swallowed and took another bite. The woods had gone silent. The birds were giving the bears a wide berth as well. If Ethan LaMont is watching us, he must be getting a hell of a laugh, I thought.

I don't know how long we waited, maybe ten minutes, then Stoner began walking slowly ahead.

"Let's take a peek," he whispered.

The bears were nowhere to be seen, but the sow had left her calling card, a pile of steaming black dung directly in our

103

path. We stepped gingerly around her leavings. Stoner picked up the pace.

■   ■   ■

We reached Half Moon Pond shortly after three. It was easy to see how it got its name; it was crescent-shaped, like it had been cut from the earth with a giant paring knife. The trail to the water dropped into a sun-splashed clearing sprinkled with white birch. Their golden leaves snapped and crackled in the warm autumn breeze. Stoner slid out of his pack and disconnected it from the little boat.

"What a beautiful spot," I said, walking down to the water's edge. The pond was perhaps half a mile from one end to the other, maybe half again as wide. A loon cruised by, a hundred yards or so off shore. I wondered if it might have seen Ethan LaMont, and would it tell us if it did?

"Let's get camp together," Stoner said. "While you're catching dinner I can sniff around, see if our boy's in the territory."

We pitched the tent, scrounged up a good supply of firewood, dug a small but serviceable latrine, and organized our gear. Then Stoner took a collapsible fishing rod from his pack.

"See that rock ledge?" he asked, pointing across the pond. "There's a deep spring hole, about twenty yards off the rocks. That's where you'll find the trout."

He snapped the rod together, attached a small spinning reel, and began threading the monofilament line. "Grab that box and hand me a couple of swivels and one of those silver spoons."

I flipped the box open. "Looks like a Lake Clear Wabbler," I said, handing him the spoon.

"You know these?" he asked.

"My grandfather and I used to troll streamer flies behind 'em," I said.

He finished rigging the rod, tying about two feet of leader material to the spoon and attaching a single gold hook. He flipped me a package of plastic worms.

"Worms?" I sneered, half joking. "Where's the sport?"

"I prefer to call them garden hackles," Stoner said with a laugh. "This ain't sport, sport. You're fishing for dinner."

He stuck the rod in a holder that was mounted to the gunwale of the canoe.

"But if it's sport you want..."

He pulled a short aluminum rod case from his pack and withdrew a four-piece fly rod.

"There's a feeder stream at the east end of the pond," he said as he assembled the delicate rod. "Later this afternoon you might see an Isonychia hatch. I'll give you some Caddis flies, too."

He attached the reel and stowed the rod and box of flies in the canoe.

"Good fishing," he chortled and headed into the woods. "Get a fire started if you're back before me."

And then he was gone.

■   ■   ■

Reaching the ledge I cast over the stern and resumed a slow paddle. When I thought the worm near the bottom, I tightened the reel's drag. Stoner had told me to zig-zag from one end of the ledge to the other. If I didn't pick up a fish, he'd suggested I move out into deeper water.

"Don't take your eyes off the tip of the rod," he'd said. "It'll just twitch, shake a little. You'll have to strike fast to hook the fish, and don't drop your paddle in the pond in the process," he'd added with a laugh.

The first couple of passes were unproductive. I wondered if Ethan LaMont was watching me, perhaps critiquing my trolling technique. A kingfisher splashed into the water. Emerging with a small fish squirming in its beak, it flew to a sagging tree limb where it swallowed its catch whole. *Bastard,* I thought. *You've probably eaten every little trout in the pond.*

I was turning the boat out just a bit when the rod tip twitched. I dropped the paddle and grabbed the rod with my right hand. Nothing. The fish was gone, or I was dragging bottom. I reeled in. The hook was clean. Someone had once written that trout are smarter in the Adirondacks. Now I believed it. I hooked on another worm and cast back into the water. The loon—I was sure it was the same one I'd seen from camp—was cruising about 30 yards off my bow. "Where are the fish?" I shouted. The loon tucked its head into the water and disappeared. *Find them yourself.*

I paddled further off the ledge, hoping to cross the spring hole. My rod tip jerked again. I was faster this time. I struck hard; the fish was hooked. It was racing to the bottom, stretching the line, which could snap at any moment. I spun the drag open. The fish ripped off another ten feet of line. When it paused momentarily I raise the rod and tightened the drag. I was retrieving some slack when my fish raced off again. This time its run was shorter. I began taking back more line. The fish fought valiantly, making another desperate rush before giving itself up to my net. It was a brook trout, two pounds or more. Its spotted flanks sparkled like shards of colored glass. Having found the spring hole, I hooked three more trout in short order. The largest had to be three pounds, easily the biggest brook trout I'd ever caught. Dinner was secured; now for some sport. I headed for the feeder stream.

Trout congregate where small streams flow into larger bodies of water. The oxygen content there is higher, and the flowing water is likely to carry flies that are easy pickings for a cruising trout. I drifted for a few minutes near the mouth of the stream, to see if any fish were feeding on the surface. Not spotting a rise, I beached the canoe and began working my way upstream on foot. I was careful not to walk too closely to the bank and spook any feeding fish. The stream took a sharp turn, which led me to a deep, shaded pool. I took a knee and scanned the surface. I was looking for any disturbance on the water. Even a dimple would point to a hungry trout slurping flies at its leisure. I waited several minutes. The pool was still. I tied on a tan-colored Caddis fly. Perhaps I could lure a trout up from deeper water by skittering the fluffy Caddis over the surface. The bank of the little stream was thick with beech and yellow birch. I remembered Pop showing me a roll cast, a way of flipping a fly onto the water when there was no space to execute a back cast. Holding the rod perpendicular to the water, I peeled some line from the reel. Then rolling the rod with my wrist, I tried to flip the fly onto the water. My first three attempts were failures, leaving most of the line draped over my head. I looked around, as if anyone were watching. I tried again, this time landing the Caddis in the middle of the pool. Gathering in some slack, I began flicking the fly across the water toward me.

The fish rose from the depths of the pool with such velocity that when it struck the Caddis it kept soaring, clearing the surface of the water by a foot or more. Then it tumbled back into the water, diving for the far side of the pool. I raised my rod, palming the reel to create some drag. The fish struggled mightily against the sting of the hook. I gave it plenty of line, but my fish soon tired. It was a small brookie, about six inches long, more brightly colored than the fish I'd taken from the pond. I quickly removed the hook and placed it gently back into the water. It darted back to the bottom of the pool as if it had been shot from a gun. I caught four more, all about the same size.

Moving upstream I located another pool. It was rimmed with massive chunks of granite. I sat down on a rock, dangling my feet just above the water. A maple leaf the color of fresh blood drifted by my toe. A large black ant was standing bravely in its cusp, the captain of its own ship. I wondered if the ant would make it to the pond, or would a gust of wind blow it into the water where it would surely be swallowed by a hungry trout? Would I find Ethan LaMont? Or would I be swallowed by the wilderness that now surrounded me? Neither the ant nor I had a ready answer.

Suddenly the air was thick with mayflies and the pool roiled with rising fish. I tied on an Isonychia, a large, gaudy fly, mostly brown with red and yellow trim, easy to follow in a swirling current or in fading light. The action was fast and furious. In twenty minutes I caught and released a dozen dazzling brook trout, brilliant in color and full of fight. But it was getting dark. I took one last cast, watching the big fly float the length of the pool without a strike. I reeled in and headed back to the canoe. The woods were uncommonly quiet. Then a twig snapped behind me. Was it the bear, or a deer, perhaps, startled by my presence? Was it Stoner, just breaking my balls? Or was it the ghost, Ethan LaMont? Nah, the Last Hermit of the Adirondacks was probably a hundred miles from Half Moon Pond.

■　　　■　　　■

I left the trout on the stringer, hanging off the stern of the canoe. Stoner would want to cook them fresh. The leaves were dry and the kindling plentiful. I got a fire going, gradually adding larger chunks of yellow birch that would settle into a nice bed of coals. The pond was mirror still, a golden eye, sparkling in the soft twilight of early evening. It was going to be a cold night. I ducked into the tent for my fleece.

It took me ten minutes or so to collect an armful of more firewood. I stacked it next to the firepit, then sat down and warmed my hands near the flames. What is it about the smell of a campfire, of wood smoke, that takes you to another place, a quiet place that somehow seems closer to the heart? The loon was back, cruising just off shore. Even in the fading light I could see its searing red eyes piercing the mist that was just rising off the water. Native Americans believed their shamans could transform themselves into winged or hoofed beings. I wondered if Ethan LaMont might have this magical power. Had he taken the form of the loon and was now drifting silently in the mist, watching my every move? I picked up a small stone and threw it into the lake. The loon dove out of sight before my errant toss hit the water.

"How was the fishing?"

I spun around. It was Stoner, standing just behind me.

"You scared the shit out of me!" I yelped.

"Shouldn't throw stones at the loons," he said with a grin.

He sat down and warmed his hands by the fire.

"Got four nice trout on the stringer," I said. "Didn't know when you'd be back so I didn't clean them."

"Well, I'm back," he replied. "I'll get some potatoes started, cook some bacon."

He flipped me a folded knife. "Stoner's rule."

"What's that?" I asked

"You catch 'em, you clean 'em."

"Any sign of LaMont?" I asked, glancing back over the pond. The loon hadn't reappeared.

"Nada," Stoner replied. "I made a circle of the pond. Found what was left of an old shanty camp. Probably his, but it hadn't been used in a couple of years. No fresh sign, that's for sure."

"So we struck out here?"

"Looks that way," he replied. "We'll head downriver in the morning."

■   ■   ■

Like the fabled Adirondack guides before him, Stoner was a master camp chef. The trout were sizzling in the skillet just minutes after I had them cleaned. He served his pan-browned trout with smashed red skin potatoes and broccoli. Dessert was a Dutch-oven baked cake and fresh-brewed, cowboy style coffee.

"Stogie?" he asked, pulling two black cheroots from his shirt pocket.

"The stogies are on me," I replied.

I ducked back into the tent for a couple of Pop's Cubans.

Stoner rolled the Montecristo over in his hand.

"This ain't no stogie, Flynn; THIS is a cigar!" He pulled a bottle of Knob Creek from his rucksack. "And THIS is bourbon!"

Tossing what was left of our coffee into the fire, we poured our bourbon and lit up the cigars. A yipping coyote, then another, took up an eerie chorus somewhere behind us.

I took a long puff from my cigar. "I thought I'd be in and out of here in a couple of days, I said. "But I've got to admit…"

"This IS fun, isn't it?" Stoner added quickly.

"Yeah, I guess it is."

"Rufus told me he could never figure out how you ended

up working in New York City, living the high life, as he put it. He said you loved it up here, talked about living here when you got out of college."

I took a sip of bourbon. "That's a long story."

"We're not going anywhere, 'til morning," Stoner replied. He placed three thick birch limbs on the fire. "That's about an hour's worth."

"I thought about being a doctor, have a small practice here in the mountains," I began. "Guess I kinda lost my bearings on the West Coast. Then I met Stephanie."

"Stephanie your wife?" Stoner asked.

"Almost," I replied, filling him in on all the gory details.

He took a long drag on his cigar. "You're lucky," he said finally.

"I should have seen it coming," I replied. "When Stephanie and I started dating..." I downed more bourbon, "her parents had a place on Park Avenue, a summer home on Martha's Vineyard. I got swept up in the glamour of it all...pretty intoxicating stuff. Maybe you're right. The mortgage meltdown probably saved my sorry ass."

"Rufus told me they canned you, even though you had nothing to do with it."

"They lost a bundle, needed to restructure."

"So are you going back...to the investment game?" Stoner asked.

"Right now I don't have a clue."

I poured more bourbon. Stoner did the same.

"Women are complicated critters," he began. "Just when you think you've got one figured out she'll bite you in the ass. Trust me, Flynn. I know."

Stoner's remark about women surprised me. Cheyenne Levine's implication about Stoner's sexual preferences may have been off base. Something wasn't making sense about this guy.

"What about you, Arlo? What's your story?" I asked.

He blew a perfect smoke ring toward the fire.

"I grew up in Malone, just north of here. Went to Syracuse on a football scholarship, but tore up a knee in my freshman year. My big time football career was over. I hung around for another year, but was so pissed about how things worked out that I split for Wyoming. Got a job as a wrangler on a ranch—I was always pretty good around horses—started guiding part-time, then was hired by one of the big outfitters to guide full-time on the Yellowstone."

"How'd you end up here, in the Adirondacks?"

"Hakeem. He left Syracuse about the same time I did. But he lit out for France. Wanted to be a chef instead of a computer geek."

"You were friends at Syracuse?" I asked.

"We grew up in Malone, been friends most of our lives. Anyway, Hakeem learned to cook in Paris, then came back, got a job in Lake Placid making good money, but, like most chefs, always wanted a place of his own. When he found what he was looking for in Lost Pond, he tracked me down and asked me to help him get it up and running. Hakeem isn't much of a carpenter. We've both been here about five years."

"So you and Hakeem are business...partners?" I asked, hoping he'd know what I was really asking.

Stoner blew another perfect smoke ring. He looked at me with a wickedly devious grin. "What is it you REALLY want to know, Flynn?"

I'd had just enough bourbon to ask. "Well, Arlo, I've been led me to believe you and Hakeem are...partners."

"Lovers, is that what you mean?" Stoner asked. He was still grinning.

"Well...yeh," I stammered.

"You got something against gay people, Flynn?"

"No, I don't. But I don't believe you are."

"Funny…" Stoner was laughing.

"What's funny?" I asked.

"Your grandfather didn't believe it either." He poured another drink.

"It's a moustache."

"A moustache? What in hell are you talking about?" I asked.

"A moustache, a disguise, a cover."

"A cover? A cover for what?"

"Tasha," Stoner replied.

"Tasha? The old fly tier's wife? What's she got to do with…oh," I stammered. "You and her…"

"You've got it, Flynn. We're the lovers. It's what you might call a creative arrangement," Stoner began. "Tasha loves old Royal…like a grandfather. She takes damn good care of him, and she'll do it 'til the day he dies. But the old fly fisherman hasn't seen a rise since gas was fifty cents a gallon."

"If he's impotent, why did she marry him? Hell, he's nearly fifty years older than she is."

"That's how Tasha got into the U.S. of A…became an American citizen. Now she's repaying her debt, so to speak, by taking care of him."

"And Royal…how's he feel about your little arrangement?"

"He's none the wiser and neither is anyone else," Stoner replied. "This way Tasha and I don't have to sneak around, we're just friends, as they say, and everyone is happy."

"Do you think that's fair to Royal?"

"I love old Royal. Do anything for him. He's getting good care, and it makes him feel like a real man to have a young woman on his arm. Like I said, everyone's happy."

"I'll be dipped," I replied.

Stoner slapped me on the shoulder. "Your grandfather thought it was a hell of an idea; in fact, it was his idea."

"You're shitting me?" I exclaimed.

"Feel better, Flynn? Now you can sleep without keeping one eye open."

We both laughed.

"For a while I thought we might be camping on Brokeback Mountain," I added.

We laughed even harder.

Chapter Ten

I woke to the spatter of rain against the walls of the tent. Stoner's sleeping bag was empty. I rolled over and poked my head out between the tent flaps. The campsite was thick with wood smoke. It was hanging in the water-sopped air like a cold Maine fog. Stoner had set up his kitchen under a tarp upwind from the fire.

"Morning, Flynn," he said cheerfully. "Get your ass in gear."

I pulled on my rain jacket and stumbled off to take a whiz. A red squirrel, sitting on a nearby stump, watched my hot pee splay off the icy rocks in an acerbic mist. I finished with a good fart, sending the squirrel dashing for cover.

"Coffee?" Stoner asked. He was already filling my mug. "Pancakes will be done in a minute."

"What's the plan?" I asked, taking my first sip. I wondered if Ethan LaMont was hunkered down out of the rain as well, or if he was on the move, already miles ahead of us.

Stoner flipped a pancake on to my plate which he'd warmed by the fire.

"Butter and syrup are on the table."

The "table" was a chunk of split maple atop four flat stones. I pulled Stoner's hunting knife from the table top and hacked off a slab of butter.

"That's real maple syrup," Stoner said. "Doc and I make up a few gallons every year." It was thick, dark and sweet.

"We'll head back to the river, move downstream," Stoner began. "If LaMont's on the Otter we might pick up his trail. If not, we'll head for the south side of the Hogback."

115

He poured another gob of batter onto the iron skillet, and then dug into his own pancake.

"What's the Hogback?" I asked.

"Geologically speaking, it's a giant-sized esker, a mile long pile of rocks left behind by the glaciers 14,000 years ago," Stoner mumbled between bites from his pancake. "The Hogback separates the Otter River from Little Buck Pond. From the south side of the Hogback, LaMont can watch the river, and he's not far from the big camps on the Osprey Chain. Once winter sets in they're easy pickings."

"And if we don't find any sign of him there?" I asked.

"We'll head for the north rim"

"Why the north rim?" I asked. "What up there?"

"From there LaMont can keep an eye on Little Buck Pond and the Algonquin Club."

"What's the Algonquin Club?" I asked.

"A seventy-five-thousand acre playground for the rich and famous," Stoner replied. "There are five club camps on Little Buck. The road from the main lodge to those camps isn't plowed. And the people who own those camps ride golf carts in February, not snowmobiles. LaMont can just move in and make himself at home."

"A club with that kind of money must have some kind of security, a caretaker at least, someone who patrols the place," I said.

"Red Meeker's been the club's caretaker for years. But he hasn't caught LaMont yet," Stoner replied. "Tell the truth I don't think he's trying very hard. LaMont's kind of a folk hero among the locals." Stoner dropped another pancake on my plate. "There's batter enough for one more."

"I'll split this one with you," I replied.

■   ■   ■

When we reached the river the rain had eased to a misting drizzle. An hour later the sun broke through; the sky cleared to a soft cerulean blue. Making our way downstream, Stoner began exploring a handful of hummocks, tiny islands hidden in a jungle of cattails through which the river meandered to the Osprey Lakes.

"Think we've got something," Stoner called back over his shoulder. I was following him up a narrow, twisting backwater that seemingly led nowhere. He climbed out of his canoe onto a hummock and disappeared into a thicket of speckled alder. I followed.

"What is it?" I asked.

We were standing in a small clearing maybe ten feet in diameter.

"Look...a firepit," Stoner replied. He picked up a small stick and flicked at the coals. A wisp of white smoke rose from the ashes.

"Holy shit," I stammered. I could feel the pancakes take a slow turn in my stomach.

"LaMont was here, last night," Stoner said, already heading back to his canoe. "I'll betcha one of those Cuban seegars he's on his way up the Hogback."

We flipped our canoes around and headed back downriver. After an hour, and a couple of false starts, Stoner found a clear channel through the marsh to the edge of the Hogback. The alders that choked the channel jingled like chimes in the soft, early afternoon breeze. Sparrows and flycatchers were everywhere, feeding on a banquet of seeds.

After paddling twenty minutes or so, the channel ended abruptly in a thick clump of cedars.

"Look, here, in the mud," Stoner said, pointing to a flat spot along the muddy bank. "I can see where he pulled his canoe out. He's here all right."

"So what do we do now?" I asked, using the moment to take a long drink of water.

"We take a random scoot."

"A what?" I asked.

"A look-see, a walk about," Stoner replied climbing from his boat. He grabbed my bow and pulled me up onto shore. "There's an old cabin site not far from here. That's where we'll make camp." We grabbed our packs and I followed Stoner into the woods.

■　　　■　　　■

"What's next?" I asked, dumping my third armload of firewood next to Stoner's improvised firepit. We'd set up camp, but had plenty of daylight left.

"We'll cover this side of the ridge, kinda crisscrossing our way from the bottom to the top," Stoner explained. "It won't be easy going, but that's why the Hermit likes it over here. Fill your water bottle. You're in for a good workout."

■　　　■　　　■

Stoner was right. The south face of the Hogback was littered with fallen trees.

"Looks like a tornado hit this place," I gasped, crawling over a shattered white pine.

"It was a derecho, actually," Stoner said, bounding over the splintered debris like a squirrel.

"A what?" I stammered, trying to keep up.

"A derecho is a mass of thunderstorms that moves in a straight line, as a single giant storm," Stoner replied. "This one slammed through here in July nineteen-ninety-five. Winds may have topped two hundred miles an hour, no one knows for sure. In just half an hour it killed three people and tore up

130,000 acres of trees."

He pulled out his water bottle. "See why LaMont likes it over here?"

Tramping westerly for several hundred yards, then moving up the ridge side twenty yards or so, and then working back in an easterly direction, we'd covered about a third of the Hogback's south face when Stoner stopped suddenly.

"What is it?" I asked.

"Something didn't look right back there."

We turned around and retraced our steps to a brush pile.

"What's the big deal?" I asked.

Stoner ran his hand over some broken limbs.

"Watch this," he said, lifting a large, fan-shaped chunk of red pine from the pile.

"Holy shit," I stammered. "LaMont's canoe?"

"That's my guess," Stoner said. "Left some fishing gear...probably going to work both sides of the Hogback...till the river freezes."

I looked around, expecting the Last Hermit of the Adirondacks to charge us wielding an ax in one hand, his rifle in the other.

"What do you think?" I asked finally.

Stoner replaced the branch.

"Let's keep moving. If he's here, it's just a question of waiting around 'til he finds you."

"Finds...us," I added.

"No, finds you," Stoner said. "I'm out of here in the morning...got a fishing client coming in."

We spent the rest of the afternoon scouring the south face. The blowdowns were so tangled, so thick we might have walked within a few feet of LaMont's camp and never seen it. Stoner, stopping frequently, would drop to a knee and peer beneath the brush. He was looking for broken twigs, matted grass, a faint trail, a sign that something—or someone—was moving in and out of the bramble. It was late afternoon when we reached the top of the Hogback. Stoner leaned back against a moss-draped boulder and took a drink.

"We may have missed something, who knows," he sighed. "Or he's down there," he added, pointing over the north side of the ridge."

"You think so?" I asked.

Stoner took another long drink, wiping the sweat from his forehead with his shirtsleeve.

"Why would he crash around in this crap if he didn't..." Stoner stopped in mid sentence.

"What is it?" I asked.

"Over there," Stoner replied, throwing a leg over a fallen tree trunk and sliding to the other side. I stumbled after him.

"Looks like the Hermit just got himself a deer," Stoner said. He was standing over a pile of animal guts and pools of dried blood.

Stoner looked around.

"See where he dragged it out, there," he said, pointing to a narrow clearing in the brush. "He killed it yesterday, I'd guess. Let's see where he went."

Ethan LaMont couldn't be far away. I was sweating like a pig but felt suddenly very cold. We paralleled the ridgeline for twenty yards or so. "Here's where he headed down, right here," Stoner said.

"How can you tell?" I asked. "I don't see a thing."

Stoner pointed to clump of pine needles about the size of my hand.

"That's dried blood, there. He's cut the deer up by now, drying some, probably storing a few choice cuts in some multimillionaire's refrigerator down there," he added, nodding toward the Algonquin Club property. "But he won't move down there 'til we get a few feet of snow." Stoner looked around. "We're about a half a mile from our camp, pretty much a straight shot from here back down the ridge."

He took a piece of red cloth from his pocket and tied it to a low hanging spruce branch. "When you walk back up here tomorrow, this is where to start your search. Look around now, get your bearings so you can find this marker in the morning."

■   ■   ■

Stoner was right. It was just about a straight line from where we'd seen our last sign of LaMont back down the south face of the Hogback. It took us about an hour to bushwhack our way back to camp. We got a fire started. I began assembling my gear for a couple of days on my own. Stoner was making sure I'd be traveling light. He put together a selection of freeze-dried foods that would only need hot water to turn them into, well, almost edible meals. Not up to Hakeem's standards, but good enough. Stoner showed me how to operate the backpack-style cook stove. There was a spring nearby. We boiled and treated a good supply of drinking water. While it was still a little daylight, Stoner went over the topo map with me and gave me a compass.

"It's basically northeast down to Little Buck Lake, then southwest up the ridge and back here," Stoner said. "If you're not back in Lost Pond in three days, I'll come looking for you," he laughed.

We got the coffee going along with a pot of boiling water for what turned out to be "pasta a la Hakeem"—a red sauce with scallops and chunks of lobster over angel hair. Cigars followed, along with some Cognac Stoner had saved for our last night. I checked my watch as we crawled into our sleeping bags. It was just past ten.

■   ■   ■

The smell of sizzling bacon lured me from a deep sleep. I unzipped the tent flap. Dawn was just breaking through the trees. Stoner had breakfast well under way.

"LaMont smells that he may join us," I muttered as I crawled from the tent pulling up my pants.

"That'd make things a whole lot easier, now wouldn't it?" Stoner said.

He emptied a bowl of scrambled eggs into the skillet.

"Let's eat. I have miles to go before I sleep, and so do you," he added with wink. We ate quickly but lingered over coffee.

"Any last minute words of wisdom…before I head off?" I asked.

Stoner looked at me with a grin. "He knows we're here."

"That's what I thought. Is that good or bad?"

"If he's curious, he won't run," Stoner replied. "If you find his camp, just sit tight. Sooner or later he'll show up."

"So where do you suggest I start?"

"The going will be a lot easier on the other side," Stoner replied. "The Big Wind didn't touch it. When you get to the top, where I left that piece of red cloth, work your way easterly for about a quarter mile and then start down toward Little Buck. Go three, four hundred yards, and that should put you just above the Palisades."

"The Palisades?" I asked.

"A rock shelf…there's some caves up there," Stoner replied.

"Caves?" I replied. "You think that's where I'll find LaMont?"

"Maybe...maybe not," Stoner added with a wink.

I finished my coffee. "See you back in Lost Pond," Stoner said over his shoulder as he pushed off in his canoe. I watched him until he rounded a sharp bend in the river.

And then he was gone.

Chapter Eleven

I'd checked my compass more than once to make sure I was on track. Even so, when I reached the top of the ridgeline I couldn't find Stoner's red cloth marker anywhere. How far off could I be? Stoner was right about one thing; the Hogback's north slope was untouched by the storm that had ripped the woods below me to shreds. The air was still, lush with the sweetness of spruce and balsam pine. I made my way easterly along the ridge for half an hour. But something was wrong. I couldn't have missed Stoner's marker by such a wide margin. So I turned around and worked my way back to where I'd started. Then I headed westerly. I hadn't gone a hundred yards when I found the mossy boulder where Stoner and I had stopped the day before. Now I had my bearings. I quickly relocated the gut pile, made my way out of the thicket, and found the tree where Stoner had tied the red cloth. It was the same tree. I was sure of it. But there was no red cloth marker. Stoner had tied it off with a stiff knot. Only a man could have undone it.

Ethan LaMont.

I was sure he was watching me now. And this time I was alone. I took a long drink of water, all the while sneaking a look around me, trying not to move my head. If LaMont was eying me from the shadows I didn't want him to know he'd rattled me so. But why did LaMont swipe Stoner's marker? Was he trying to make it tougher on me, throw me off the trail, or was that his way of saying *hey, I know you're here. Now try to find me.*

Following Stoner's advice, I moved along the ridgeline

several hundred yards. Then I began descending the Hogback's north side. But I couldn't help looking over my shoulder, more than once, wondering if the Last Hermit of the Adirondacks was right behind me. If he were, would he spring some sort of trap? Or would he get his kicks watching me get hopelessly lost? A spruce grouse exploded into the air, scaring the crap out of me. The pines were now so thick I had to crawl on my hands and knees to keep the low-hanging limbs from snaring my pack. A shrew scurried past my nose, terrified no doubt that a monster was invading its turf. I crawled for ten or fifteen minutes, then at last broke into a clearing sprinkled with birch trees. I welcomed the chance to stand on my feet again. The pine needle forest floor gradually gave way to lichen blanketed rocks. Then I walked out onto a wide overlook.

Little Buck Lake, perhaps a half a mile away, glistened like a blue pearl in the high morning sun. I took a long drink of water and a chew of Stoner's jerky. He was probably halfway back to Lost Pond by now. I sat down on a rock and waited, wondering if Ethan LaMont might just creep up behind me and touch me on the shoulder. I gave him fifteen minutes or so. Ethan LaMont, of course, was a no-show. It was early in the game that I now knew he was playing with me. And I was losing. I got back up, tightened my pack, and lowered myself over a gentle ledge onto the rocks below. I was sure I'd found the Palisades. The densely wooded terrain had given way to a lichen-coated ridge of granite pocked with pools of snowmelt. I inched my way along, crawling up and over the massive rocks, discovering a number of wide fissures, but no caves, no sign of the phantom hermit. What now? I stripped off my pack and let the warm sun massage my aching shoulders and back. A raven swept over my head, riding the wind like a surfer hugging a rolling wave. I watched it make a slow, arching loop.

Cr-r-ruck...cr-r-ruck.

Surprisingly, it settled onto a nearby chunk of stone.

Cr-r-ruck...cr-r-ruck.

It cocked its head. Then it flew to the top of a muffin-shaped boulder, this one about twenty yards down the ledge. It cocked its head again.

Cr-r-uck...cr-r-ruck.

The raven flew off again, coming to rest a bit further down the ledge.

Cr-r-uck...cr-r-ruck.

It was almost as if the raven wanted me to follow it. What the hell, I thought. I didn't have a better plan. I picked up my pack and scrambled down the rocks, skinning both my knees along the way. I was within a few feet of the raven when it rose suddenly into the air and disappeared below the ledge. I chased after it, to the edge of the rock shelf. And there it was.

"Son of a bitch!" I shouted. It was Stoner's marker.

The ragged strip of red cloth he'd tied to the tree limb near the top of the ridge was tucked beneath a stone about the size of a basketball. Could the raven have snatched the marker from the tree, brought it here, and somehow found the strength to move a rock easily fifty times its weight?

"LaMont!" I screamed.

There was no answer but for the distant echo of my desperate cry. I turned slowly. Was he standing behind me, grinning from ear to ear, or perhaps preparing to shove me over the ledge?

The raven had left me very much alone.

What now? I took another drink of water and checked my skinned knees. The bleeding had stopped. I dabbed the wounds with a clean piece of my handkerchief, rolled my pant legs back down, and began working my way along the narrow ledge. If LaMont were baiting me with Stoner's marker, I'd swallowed his hook whole.

Another fifty yards found me on a narrow ledge no wider than the length of my size eleven boot. Then I made a mistake; I looked down. It had to be more than two hundred feet to the rock pile below. My head was spinning. I closed my eyes, breathing deeply, trying to summon the courage—or foolhardiness—to continue on. Water was now oozing like oil from a run of thread-thin fissures in the rocks, making the footing even more treacherous. At least Stoner would know where to look for my body. I crept along for another hundred feet, only to find myself stuck at a dead end. There was no where to go but down, or back where I'd come from. Then I caught a whiff of wood smoke. The camps at Little Buck Lake were a good mile away. And Stoner had told me they were pretty much closed up for winter. I scanned the rocks.

Jesus Christ!

Wisps of white smoke were curling up from a thin crevasse in the rocks just to my right.

LaMont's camp!

I was sure of it, but what now? There was a wedge of rock, about ten feet below me. I could jump. I could also break an ankle, a leg, or worse. But I couldn't turn around either.

So I jumped.

The crash landing wasn't pretty. My knees buckled beneath me and I rolled like a log over the jagged stones. Luckily I was able to grab a handhold before tumbling off the ledge and spamming myself all over the rocks below. I lay still for a moment, catching my breath, wiggling my toes…moving my legs and then my arms. Luckily, nothing was broken.

I sat up. The view from the ledge was breathtaking. Framed through a grove of shimmering birch trees, Marcy, Algonquin and Haystack, highest of the Adirondack High

Peaks, appeared close enough to touch. But of course they were miles still to the east. An eagle soaring lazily overhead turned westerly, probably disappointed it wouldn't be picking my carcass clean. I staggered to my feet. The smell of wood smoke was now overwhelming.

I turned very slowly around.

The campfire was perhaps 30 feet back into the rocks. The smoke was curling up through a series of fissures in the granite ceiling, thus dispersing any tell-tale sign.

I'd leapt into the mouth of LaMont's cave.

There appeared to be no way out.

I stripped off my pack and cautiously made my way into the wide crack in the rock wall. Strips of meat were hanging from birch poles that were arranged tepee-fashion over the fire, most likely venison from LaMont's recent kill. The cave's walls were lined with wooden crates of dried foodstuffs, cooking gear, assorted tools, extra boots and clothing. A sleeping bag was spread over a thick bed of fresh pine boughs in back of the fire pit. Hanging from a clothesline near the fire were a pair of green wool pants, red long johns, and a red and black checked wool shirt. There was a crude but functional three-shelf pantry of canned fruits and vegetables, bags of salt and sugar, several cans of coffee and assorted condiments. Three unlit oil lamps were hanging from iron spikes driven into the cave's granite walls. LaMont's rocking chair, crafted of stick wood, sat next to a four-tier birch-planked bookshelf. The Last Hermit's library included Thoreau, Jack London, Barry Lopez and John McPhee. This clearly was no hastily erected brush shanty; this was Ethan LaMont's base camp. I walked back into the sunlight and began rubbing the smoke from my watering eyes.

"So who are you, and what the fuck do you want?"

I twisted around. The voice was curt and cold, its edge as

sharp as a skinner's knife. I squinted back into the cave. But I saw nothing.

"LaMont...Ethan LaMont?" I stammered.

"Never heard of him," came the crusty reply.

"You're Ethan LaMont, U.S. Army, retired."

"Who told you that?"

"State police have identified you. It was in the newspapers. You are Ethan LaMont...aren't you?"

"I'm asking the questions. Who the FUCK are you?"

"My name is Ryan Flynn," I stammered. "I'm not a cop."

"No shit, sailor."

The Last Hermit of the Adirondacks stepped into the flickering light of the campfire. Ethan LaMont was a sinewy six feet. His hair, long and black with rivulets of gray, just touched his square, muscular shoulders. I put him in his mid-sixties. He was hatchet-faced, with high, sharp cheekbones. His skin was the color of well-seasoned cherry wood. He wore leggings and a shirt of tanned buckskin. A wolf's head forged of silver and about the size of a fifty-cent piece hung from his neck on a choker of blue and yellow beads.

"You...you led me here...you and the raven..." I said.

LaMont, surprisingly, smiled. He stepped from the cave. His searing emerald eyes bore into me like a wildcat.

"Raven is my brother," he replied, flipping a small stone off the ledge. "You went to a lot of trouble finding me, you and whoever that was who left you this morning."

"You WERE watching us, weren't you?" I replied.

"Who is he?"

"Arlo Stoner. He's a guide who works out of Lost Pond."

"I've seen him enough, but never knew his name," LaMont replied.

"Stoner thought I'd have better luck finding you if I came alone," I replied.

"This Arlo Stoner is a smart man," he replied. "I might have shot the both of you."

I think he was smiling, but I couldn't be sure. He flung another stone. "You handle a fly rod pretty well."

"You were there, too?" I gasped

"I picked you up at Rocky Brook," LaMont began. "It was pretty clear you were looking for me. You kind of piqued my curiosity. Raven told me your medicine is strong."

"I don't know if I'd put it quite that way," I replied.

"So what brings you up here, Ryan Flynn?" LaMont replied. "I hope you're not some goddamned reporter, a writer looking for a story, are you?"

"No. I've got the story. But you can help me with the ending."

He looked me over, the intensity in his flashing eyes forcing me to blink.

"You are Ethan LaMont, aren't you?" I asked again.

He smiled.

"I am. Let's have a drink."

He walked back into the cave and returned with a bottle of Jack Daniels and two blue metal cups.

"Thank you, Hawley."

"Hawley?" I asked.

"Hawley Robeson, Trans World Oil," LaMont replied, pointing down toward Little Buck and the Algonquin property. "Paid him a visit last week, but old Hawley wasn't there," LaMont added with a soft laugh.

He poured my drink and then attended to his own.

"So, Flynn, what's the story?"

I took a long swallow of Hawley Robeson's bourbon.

"How's your Adirondack history?" I asked.

"Try me," LaMont replied.

"Erik von Koenig…ever heard of him?"

130

"He built the first railroad to cross the North Country…owned nearly a quarter of a million acres…blew his brains out back in the twenties." LaMont gave me a cold stare. "Shit, you're just another goddamned treasure hunter."

He began walking back into the cave.

"Your grandfather was Louie LaMont," I said.

He stopped. "So? That's not exactly breaking news."

"Your grandfather drowned in Lake Champlain," I continued. "His body was found November seventh, nineteen-twenty-eight."

"Like I said, that's not news either," LaMont replied.

"Your grandfather worked for von Koenig at his Eagle's Nest estate. He was the rail baron's most trusted guide."

"You came all the way up here to tell me that?"

"Your grandfather helped pulled off the biggest heist in Adirondack history."

"What the fuck are you talking about?"

"You might want to sit down for this."

Ethan LaMont took a swig of his bourbon. "I'll stand right here, sailor."

"Did you know the day your grandfather's body was discovered was the same day that Erik von Koenig murdered his aide, Aharon Friedman, set a torch to his mansion, and then took his own life?" I asked.

"So?" LaMont asked.

"Your grandfather was crossing Lake Champlain to Vermont when he must have capsized and drowned. He'd moved your grandmother and their son, Travis—your father—to a cabin outside Starksboro, Vermont, three weeks before Erik von Koenig shot his aide and subsequently took his own life. Your father was just sixteen at the time."

I thought I saw LaMont's eyes narrow. I hoped so. If he didn't believe what I was about to tell him it was going to be a long walk back to Lost Pond.

"Who the hell are you?"

"I AM Ryan Flynn," I replied. "My grandfather was Rufus Flynn. He lived in Lost Pond. About six months ago, he was diagnosed with incurable cancer. He died a couple of weeks ago. It appears, shortly before his death, he'd solved the von Koenig mystery."

LaMont sat down and poured us both more bourbon. "Keep talking."

I told him everything Pop had learned, sparing no detail.

"You're not saying…" LaMont interrupted.

"The choir boy was Adolph Hitler."

"Jesus Christ," he stammered, taking a drink of bourbon.

"Aharon Friedman, von Koenig's treasurer, enlisted your grandfather to prevent the shipping of von Koenig's wealth to Hitler's Third Reich," I continued. "Louie LaMont jumped from the train near the Otter River, stashed millions of dollars in diamonds—somewhere—and then lit out for Vermont."

"But my grandfather never made it," LaMont added.

"When von Koenig discovered Friedman's role in the plot, he shot him, set fire to his mansion, and then put a 45-caliber bullet in his brain."

"A fascinating story," LaMont said. "But my grandfather, this Aharon Friedman and von Koenig all ended up dead. Where's the proof what you're saying actually happened the way you're telling it?"

"I thought you might ask." I grabbed my pack. LaMont's hand moved ever so slightly for the bone-handled knife sheathed to his belt. He trusted no one.

"Read this," I said, handing him Friedman's confession. "It's a copy, but it's the proof you asked for."

LaMont, sipping at his bourbon, read the letter once, and then read it again.

"Who else knows about this?"

"A man named Doc Ingram, and a woman, Megan Seagar."

LaMont raised a bushy eyebrow. "Who the hell are they?"

"They live in Lost Pond. They're on our side."

"Our side?" he replied. He gazed down at Friedman's confession again. "Do you think I know what my grandfather might have done with von Koenig's diamonds?"

"No, I don't. But I thought you might want to help me find them."

LaMont broke out laughing.

"Why would I do that?" he replied. "I live in a cashless society. Find the diamonds yourself."

He turned his back on me, staring off toward the High Peaks.

"It's not about the diamonds," I said, trying not to sound like I was pleading. "It's about your grandfather...and Aharon Friedman. They died to keep millions of dollars out of the hands of Adolph Hitler. If you'll help me, their deaths will not have been in vain."

LaMont looked back at me. "How's that?"

"Does the name Simeon Leache mean anything to you?" I asked.

"Simeon Leache? His goddamned helicopter disturbs my peace. And that gilded palace he built...drilled his own gas wells up there and polluted a damn fine trout stream in the process. Son of a bitch," LaMont added.

"He's a wacko radical radio broadcaster now. Pretty scary guy," I added.

"I haven't exactly been listening to the radio lately," LaMont added with a sly smile. "What does Simeon Leache have to do with whatever it is you're trying to suck me into?"

I quickly summarized the relationship between William

and Marshall College, Lost Pond, and the Friends of George I. Gurdjieff. Then I explained Leaches' efforts to purchase Lost Pond for the purpose of establishing what would essentially be a neo-Nazi training school.

LaMont tugged at his beard. "I think I see where you're going with this. What are these diamonds worth again?"

"Two, three million, maybe more," I replied.

"And what's Leache offering the college?"

"Ten million," I replied.

LaMont reached over and replenished my bourbon.

"I'd say you're a little short, sailor."

"Help me find the diamonds. I'll do the rest."

"The rest?"

"The diamonds can be leveraged to twice, maybe three times their value," I replied.

"You're still short," LaMont added.

"The Adirondack Preservation Society has already agreed to accept, shall we say, an anonymous multimillion dollar grant for the purpose of preserving forever the hamlet of Lost Pond," I began. "The Society can raise the difference in a heart beat, and the college has already agreed to accept its offer, albeit a dollar above Leaches' bid. He'll never know what hit him," I added.

"Where is Simeon Leache getting his money?" LaMont asked. "Ten million is just the beginning...he'll need a hell of lot more to build this institute of his."

"Leache has a silent partner, an oil czar named Zubkov who reportedly has ties to the Russian mafia."

LaMont's face tightened. "Vladimir Zubkov?"

"You know the name?" I stammered.

LaMont topped off his bourbon. "Major Vladimir Zubkov," he said at last.

"Major?" I asked.

"Flynn, I guess I've got a story for you," LaMont began. "I was a pretty fair athlete in high school, in Vermont, and a good student, too. I got an appointment to the Naval Academy, then on to the Marines, special ops training, and two duty tours in Vietnam. After the war I was assigned to a unit so secret two Presidents didn't know it existed...for their own good. Plausible deniability they call it."

"What exactly did you do?" I asked.

"The nation's business," LaMont replied. "I killed people, foreign nationals the CIA targeted as threats to the United States of America. There was a mission in Moscow in 1989. My team was sent in to extract an Agency asset—a mole we had inside the KGB. Zubkov was running the KGB's counter-intelligence operations. The mission was a cluster fuck from the get-go. Zubkov knew we were coming. To this day I believe he had his own sources embedded in our intelligence operations. We ended up killing ten innocent people. Six were just kids...kids who Zubkov made sure were in our line of fire. No one outside our two governments ever heard about it."

LaMont took a long sip of bourbon. "My military career was over. I took the fall for a mission that was doomed from the beginning."

"What happened after that?" I asked. "I mean it's been...what...twenty years?"

"I left the Corps, did some guiding in Alaska, commercial fishing out of Homer," LaMont replied. "Loved it, but my roots are here. So I came back, went off the res as they say."

He walked to the ledge and gazed for a moment over the mountains, now painted in the crimson glow of late afternoon.

"Vladimir Zubkov, eh? Count me in."

Chapter Twelve

LaMont nudged my shoulder with his boot.

"Rise and shine."

I rolled out of my sleeping bag. It was just past five. LaMont handed me a cup of steaming black coffee. The soft light of a false dawn was dancing across the mouth of the cave. My head felt like it was jammed into the jaws of a vice. We'd polished off the bourbon. And after a dinner of venison stew, LaMont had produced a bottle of Cognac, no doubt lifted from an unsuspecting Algonquin Club member. We'd talked half the night. Ethan LaMont embraced a world beyond most anyone's experiences, well beyond the demands of modern life. His was a world of spirit and vision, of fierce independence. He lived in harmony with nature, living off the land more or less—he didn't have his own still so he helped himself to others' "beverages." He was also incredibly aware of the mess the rest of us were making of our planet. My sense was that he was a soldier waiting for his next mission. Now, with a chance to even a personal score and finish what his grandfather had started, Ethan LaMont just might have found the mission he'd been waiting for.

■　　■　　■

After a breakfast of hot oatmeal and cave-baked bran muffins, we packed enough food for three days.

"What's the plan?" I asked as LaMont was stuffing our sleeping bags into a waterproof bag.

"Well bushwhack our way off the Hogback to the rail line," he replied. "That's a couple of miles northwest of here. I keep a handcar stashed there. We'll ride it south. That will be a lot quicker than backtracking down the north branch of the Otter River. There's an old logging road north of Lost Pond. We can take it to the Otter's east branch."

"And you have a canoe stashed there, too?" I joked.

"You're catching on to the Hermit's secret tricks," LaMont replied with a wide smile. "The east branch flows all the way to Lake Champlain, where my grandfather was headed. So are we."

"What are we looking for, exactly?" I asked.

"We'll know it when we see it."

■　　■　　■

There was no trail, but Ethan LaMont instinctively found the easiest route through the unbroken woods. We avoided gullies we couldn't jump and blow downs that we couldn't climb. It took just two hours to reach to old rail line.

"Give me a hand," he said, taking off his pack and peeling back the branches of a small brush pile. LaMont had hidden the handcar well, taking the added precaution of securing it to a tree with a chain and padlock.

"I'll take the heavy end," he said opening the lock.

We lifted the contraption up onto the rails. It was perhaps ten feet long, built of two by fours and plywood. There was a small gasoline engine mounted toward the rear. A series of pulleys and belts drove power to all four steel wheels which fit over the rails.

I loaded on our gear.

"Jump on, and we'll fire this bugger up," LaMont chuckled.

He yanked the starting cord once, then again. The engine sputtered to life.

"The motor's from an old John Deere garden tractor," LaMont said. He adjusted the choke. "Let her warm up a minute."

"I saw some hunters on one of these when Megan and I were hiking up to the Overlook," I said.

"Yeh, probably the Jersey Bucks."

"The who?"

"It's a deer-hunting club, bunch of guys from New Jersey. They set up a tent camp every year on Whipple Pond...do more drinking than hunting."

The motor was running smoothly now. LaMont engaged the hand clutch and we lurched forward.

"How fast will this thing go?" I asked.

"Twenty, twenty-five maybe, fast enough."

"Is it safe? I mean, this railroad's been abandoned for how long?"

"About forty years," LaMont replied. "But it was built well, mostly by hand, and completed in less than two years...quite a feat in its day."

The little car was picking up speed. Rounding a long curve we startled a small flock of wild turkeys feeding along the edge of the tracks. One by one they lumbered into the air, disappearing into the trees on both sides of the rail bed.

"This is a snowmobile trail in the winter, so it's kept in pretty good shape," LaMont continued. "There's talk of reopening the railroad for tourists, leaf peepers, that sort of thing, but someone's going to have to spend a ton to make this safe for trains to run on it again."

He reached into his pack and tossed me a small zip-lock bag.

"Jerky?"

I pulled out a stick the size of a small cigar and took a chew.

He smiled. "Last year's deer…one of 'em."

Listening to the rumble of LaMont's contraption rolling down the old tracks conjured up images from another time, when grand steam engines, their boilers belching plumes of black smoke, thundered over the same rails, moving logs and ore, the rich and the famous, and common folk, too, across the Great North Woods.

"Sparks from those early steam engines set the woods on fire," LaMont said as if he'd been reading my mind. "The village of Tupper Lake was about burned off the map. Plenty of wrecks, too. Many a good man died along this line."

The tracks descended slightly. We crossed a wide bog. A pair of wood ducks jumped off the water. Zigzagging their way through a cluster of dead trees, they soon were out of sight.

LaMont was cutting back on the throttle.

"What's wrong?" I asked.

He was standing now, shading his eyes with his hands, peering down the tracks.

"Beavers have got the culvert jammed again."

The tracks ahead disappeared into a pond the color of my morning coffee, emerging some fifty yards on the other side.

"Can we make it through?" I asked.

"Yeah, just don't want to hit it going too fast."

LaMont eased his engine to a near idle. We chugged into the water which quickly rose over the wheels and was soon lapping at the plywood platform. Tree stumps rose from the ink water like medieval spikes, their tips gnawed to fine points by the buck-toothed engineers who built and maintained the pond.

"Industrious little bastards, aren't they?" LaMont chuckled.

Luckily the water didn't get any deeper. We emerged

from the overflow and LaMont opened the throttle. The marsh gave way to lush clumps of cedar. Then the rails rose into a dense stand of white pines that hugged both sides of the tracks. A startled spruce grouse, then another, darted down the tracks in front of us. We continued on for perhaps ten minutes, the evergreens easing into a mix of hardwoods, mostly beech and yellow birch. Then LaMont began slowly pulling back on the throttle.

"The end of the line," he said. "Trail's just up ahead."

The tracks entered a dense thicket of brambles and blow downs. LaMont pulled back on the break and hopped off.

"Let's park this bugger," he said, heading into a thicket of sumac. LaMont's "garage" was barely a clearing concealed in the thick underbrush. We pulled away a pile of brush and tree branches. Then, lugging the machine into the woods, we quickly hid it from view.

"Saddle up," he said, strapping on his pack back.

I grabbed the waterproof bag. "I don't see any trail."

"Follow me."

We pushed our way several hundred feet through a tangle of sumac and red cedar to the remnants of a road, a weedy clearing choked with cedar seedlings and knee-high grass.

"Old logger's road," LaMont said.

It led into a forest of conifers thick with ferns and mosses. We trudged on. The leaf-covered humus underfoot gave way to a soil more sand than earthy loam. I could hear the rush of water. LaMont veered off the path and into the woods. We'd walked perhaps twenty yards, when he stopped and began peeling away another brush pile.

"Our canoe," he said with a sly smile.

Like the smaller ones Stoner and I had used, it was made of Kevlar. But this one was large enough for both of us and our gear. He flipped it over. Two paddles were strapped to

140

floor.

"Kinda surprised you've got a two-man canoe," I said. "Thought you traveled alone."

"Pretty observant there, Flynn," LaMont replied. "I liberated this a year ago from someone who never used it. I can handle it fine, and it's big enough to carry a deer, equipment, when I need to."

Grabbing one of the canoe's thwarts he raised the boat to his shoulders and we turned back toward the trail. It descended down a steep hillside, crossed a small, rock-strewn feeder stream, and then broke into a sun-warmed clearing.

We'd reached the fork of the Otter River. Its west branch was a rushing swirl of tumbling, boulder strewn water. Clumps of yellow birch sprouted from the tops of the rocks like stalks of sickly corn, the trees' roots clutching to stone like the fingers of a pitcher ready to throw a fastball high and hard. In contrast, the Otter's east branch was open and wide, flowing like a giant rivulet of maple syrup under a crisp, cloud-free autumn sky.

"Where in hell are we, anyway?" I asked.

LaMont laughed.

"The trestle's only a mile upstream," he replied. "If my grandfather did jump from that train and was headed for Lake Champlain, he'd have come right by here."

LaMont looked out over the water for a moment, then tossed our gear into the canoe.

"But where did he stop to stash the diamonds? That is THE question, eh, Flynn?"

He slid the canoe into the water. I climbed into the bow seat and he pushed us off.

The current was deceiving. It was more powerful than it looked, carrying us downstream with little effort on the paddle. For the first mile or so we wound through a wide, wetland prairie of cattails and pickerelweed. An osprey swept over our heads, hitting the water talons first. It emerged into the air with a wiggling fish and flew off down the river. Blue herons were fishing, too. Some stood like lawn statues in the backwashes, watching us pass while others lifted gracefully from the shallows, gliding off ahead of us, only to be roused again by our passing. Black spruce leaned out over the water, their roots barely hanging on in the wet, soft earth. I breathed deeply. The marsh was a gumbo of aromas, all thick, pungent and sweet. Raucous flocks of blackbirds filled the air, and the tall grass teemed with flycatchers and swamp sparrows dining on ripened seeds.

"What are we looking for?" I asked.

"Higher ground," LaMont replied.

I noticed the marsh was giving way to more black spruce and tamarack.

"We've got some rapids up ahead, no big deal, but pay attention," LaMont continued. When I say right, paddle right, and paddle hard. When I say left, well, you get the picture. There are some rocks, and the current gets a little tricky," he added.

The river began to narrow. The current was picking up speed. I could hear the low roar of the rapids just ahead.

Then we dove into the swirl.

"Right paddle!"

I switched sides and dug into a churning swirl of yellowish brown foam. We slid past a mossy boulder big enough to split the stream in half. A pair of mergansers splashed off a quiet eddy near shore. They raced downstream ahead of us. The rocks around us were splayed with blotches of red and green paint, the calling cards of less skillful boatmen that bore witness to the river's treachery.

"Left Flynn, left!" LaMont shouted "You gotta pay

attention."

We threaded our way between two jagged shards of granite.

"Right, Flynn! Right!"

Switching sides, I bashed the side of the canoe with my paddle.

You dunce, I thought.

We swept past a fallen spruce and then dropped into another swirling run of angry water.

"Right, Flynn, right! Left, hard now!"

And then it was over. I wiped the sweat from my forehead.

"Fun, eh Flynn?" LaMont was laughing from his stern seat.

The river widened again. Tamarack morphed into paper birch and mountain ash. A kingfisher dove into the water just off our bow. He missed, emerging from the water empty-handed, so to speak. We watched a pair of playful mink darting among the rocks. They stopped to watch us slide silently past them, but soon resumed their romp along the river bank. We paddled on for a mile or so. The river took a lazy left turn. While the south shore remained pretty much wooded, the trees on the north side receded into a steep, boulder-scattered ridge.

"Glaciers dumped these rocks as the ice receded north," LaMont said. "Let's do a little recon."

He turned the canoe toward shore.

"This is the first ground I've seen where my grandfather might have found a place to stash the goods."

LaMont drove the canoe into a sandbank. I jumped out and pulled us ashore. We scrambled up into the rocks. It felt good to move my legs again.

"What are we looking for, I mean, what more than high

ground?" I asked.

LaMont grabbed my hand and pulled me up onto a rock-strewn ledge.

"Deep crevasses between the rocks...maybe a pile of rocks that doesn't quite look natural...like someone piled them up," he replied. "We can cover this area faster if we split up."

LaMont headed off to the south while I worked my way northerly. We zigzagged back and forth for more than two hours.

We found nothing.

"What's next?" I asked, climbing back into the canoe.

"My grandfather could have stopped anywhere," LaMont replied, pointing off into the thick cedars that lined both sides of the river. "He could have stuffed them in the hollow of a tree, dug a pit and marked it with some sign...who the hell knows."

"This is kind of a wild goose chase," I admitted, "but it's worth a try. I really appreciate your help."

"My sense is my grandfather would have kept heading downstream, wanting to get as far away from the scene of his crime as possible," LaMont said finally.

We paddled on. The river narrowed again into a series of short but roiling rapids. We ran them without incident.

"What about those rocks...up there?" I asked, pointing to a ledge of granite that rose over a quiet pool just ahead of us.

"That's our next stop," LaMont replied. "Worth a look-see."

We continued downstream about a hundred yards, beaching the canoe on a pencil-thin sand bar. After wading a shallow eddy we headed up into the woods, a riotous palette of crimson reds, pale yellows and amber browns. LaMont stopped and ran his hand over a scarred tree trunk.

"Bear...they love beechnuts," he said.

He bent down and picked up a black, square-tipped feather.

"Turkey like 'em, too."

Climbing the ridge and now more into the open, the sugar maples and beech yielded to clumps of quaking aspen and paper birch, trees that thrive in the warm sun. From the top we could see the river unfolding beneath us. LaMont pulled a water bottle from his fanny sack and took a long drink. I was about to do the same when he grabbed my arm.

"Quick, follow me."

"What the hell is it?" I asked.

I didn't have to wait for his answer. Now I heard it, too.

Womp...womp...womp.

We ducked into a wide crack in the rocks.

"Keep low," he said. "Leache's compound is north of here, maybe ten miles as the crow flies. Should have expected he'd be flying over us sooner or later."

The black helicopter, probably the same one I'd seen at Lost Pond, roared over the ridge top. We waited until it was out of sight.

"Probably over-reacting, but why take a chance," LaMont said as we crawled out into the sunlight. "Some interesting nooks and crannies up here...let's poke around some."

We followed the same routine, each covering about half the ridgeline. Near the entrance to one promising opening I found some small animal bones and chunks of blood-matted hair...the den of a fox, no doubt, or perhaps a coyote.

I moved on.

There was a wide ledge just below me. I crawled down between the rocks and discovered the mouth of a cave. I wondered if I should explore it on my own or call LaMont. I decided not to waste his time. It was probably a dead-end. I pulled out my flashlight and slowly made my way in. The remnants of an old campfire were scattered about the rock floor. Could Louie LaMont have stopped here nearly a century ago? Or was it a Mohawk fire, a hunter party escaping the ravages of a storm, perhaps, or hiding from Huron enemies? But for the old firepit, the cave was bare. I crawled out and met LaMont about where we'd started our search.

He'd found nothing. I told him about my discovery.

"My grandfather may have camped in the cave, but he didn't hide the diamonds here," LaMont said after checking the cave out himself. We headed back toward the river. "Let's keep moving downstream—closer to Lake Champlain and Vermont."

■   ■   ■

We'd paddled on for another hour, mostly over quiet water, spooking small flocks of wood ducks and mallards from their resting areas. Then LaMont turned the canoe toward a wide stretch of sand on the south shore of the river.

"What's here?" I asked.

"Camp," he replied. "We've covered as much ground as we can today."

The land rose sharply toward the summit of what LaMont told me was Morgan's Peak. I could see the tracks of several deer in the soft sand. I jumped out and yanked the canoe onto the beach. LaMont tossed me our gear.

"Let's get busy on the Goose."

"The what?" I asked.

"The Mountain Goose, the *sapin* of the French-Canadians, *cho-kho-tung* to the Mohawk people."

Clearly amused at my blank stare, LaMont broke into a laugh. He snapped off the branch of a fallen yellow birch.

Working first with his hatchet, and then his knife, he turned out a forked stick about five feet long.

"Follow me," he said, folding the knife and stuffing it into his pocket.

We climbed perhaps twenty yards, to the edge of a thick stand of sweet balsam. LaMont began snapping off the wide, low-hanging branches.

"Wouldn't it be easier to cut them off?" I asked.

"Hit 'em with an ax and they'll just snap back at you," LaMont replied. "Use a knife and you'll end up with a fistful of blisters. Watch this."

He grabbed a limb. His thumb was on top of the branch and was pointing toward the tip of the bough. Then, pressing down with his thumb he twisted the branch, snapping it off like a stem of asparagus.

"Here, you try it," he said.

After a couple of fruitless twists and turns I got the hang of it. When LaMont said we had enough, he bundled the boughs and strung them on the forked stick much as he would a string of fish, the butts of each bundle pointing in opposite directions. He then slung the stick of boughs over his shoulder and we returned to our campsite.

"That's the Goose," LaMont said, dropping the bundle, "now for the rest of our shelter."

I followed him back into the woods where he'd hidden a stack of pre-cut poles inside a hollow log. It took us a couple of trips to carry them all back to camp. In a matter of minutes LaMont had erected the frame of a lean-to.

"This was called an Adirondack Camp, in the early days," LaMont said, tying half a dozen cross poles to support the roof.

"Wouldn't it be easier just to sleep in a tent?" I asked.

He laid the last of the roof poles in place.

"That wouldn't be art, would it?"

"Art? What's that got to do with it?" I asked.

"Anyone can sleep in a tent," the Last Hermit of the Adirondacks replied as he began laying the boughs we'd cut over the lean-to's roof. He started at the bottom, working his way up, overlapping each subsequent row slightly over the other.

"My life is my art," he continued. "This shelter, for example; I've built hundreds of 'em. No two are ever the same. They're like paintings. An artist can paint the same scene a dozen times, but the composition, the flow of light, the blending of colors and layering of paint on canvas will be never be precisely the same. Living in rhythm with nature, working everyday with natural materials, preparing meals from what the woods provides us, from fish and game...see what I mean? Every day I create a work of art from my daily living. Thoreau was right."

"Right about what?" I asked.

"Most men live lives of quiet desperation," he replied, pointing a long finger in my general direction.

LaMont wove the last boughs of the roof into place. Our mattresses were next. We spread a layer of larger boughs on the ground, shingling them so that the tips pointed toward the head of the bed and overlapping the butts.

"Make it thick enough, soft like your favorite couch at home, LaMont said. "Sleeping in a shelter of pine boughs is a privilege, a joy few people ever experience."

As I worked, every piece fit naturally, snugly together. It struck me how LaMont's life and the lives of the Friends in Lost Pond were bound by the same reverence for the natural world, for the materials the earth provided. And now the Last Hermit of the Adirondacks might be the Friends' last hope.

■   ■   ■

In another hidden cache LaMont produced a well-scorched black iron cooking pot, tin dishes, utensils and a coffee pot. Then he fashioned his cooking range from a crosspole supported by two forked stakes driven into the sand over the fire pit.

"Next you'll pull a microwave from some hollow log," I joked.

LaMont laughed. "I travel light, but eat well."

He tossed me a book of stick matches. "Get the fire started. I'll get dinner together."

While I gathered up dry kindling, LaMont was cutting up potatoes, carrots and onions, which he tossed in a pot with chucks of venison and some gravy he'd brought along in a plastic water bottle. A pair of inquisitive mergansers cruised by. They were eyeing us suspiciously. Then the drake suddenly disappeared beneath the water, quickly followed by its mate. The kindling crackled under my match. I added chunks of dry wood and soon a fine flame was dancing in the stone-lined pit. The sun was dipping behind the mountains, turning the sky into a warm, light purple glaze.

"Stir the stew now and then while I get some coffee started," LaMont said. I watched as he added half a dozen heaping tablespoons of coffee to a pot of water he'd scooped from the river. After bringing it to a roiling boil, he set it to the side of the fire to simmer.

"It's my Otter River Blend," he said with a wry smile. "You won't find it at Starbucks."

He reached into his rucksack and handed me a pint of Jack Daniels. "Have a drink. You've earned it today."

I took a long, satisfying swallow.

"We haven't exactly struck it rich," I said, handing him

back the bottle. He gazed out over the river and took a swallow.

"Ye of little faith," he chortled, taking a long swig himself.

■   ■   ■

The venison stew was ready half an hour later. The meat was tender and savory, while the carrots and onions still had a snap to them. LaMont had brought along chunks of seeded rye bread to soak up the gravy. I ate a second helping while my guide poured two steaming mugs of coffee.

"Cream or sugar?" he joked, spiking his coffee with a splash of bourbon.

"As long as it's Jack Daniels," I replied.

The coffee was scalding hot, but LaMont's Otter River Blend tasted so good I sipped away.

"This hermit life, living off the land, alone," I began. "Will you ever go back?"

LaMont picked up a small, flat stone and skipped it out over the river.

"Back to what, your world, Flynn? I don't think so."

"Please don't misunderstand me," I replied. "I appreciate what you said, about your life being your work of art, but you're an educated man...you could make a difference."

"Yeh...and I've learned plenty," he laughed.

He skipped another stone out into the river.

"Nothing in life is permanent, Flynn, absolutely nothing. My coming to the Adirondacks, living in this manner...I hope to awaken my spirit to a new purpose...or not...perhaps this is it. A vibrant and full life is a continuing quest, a spiritual journey into the wilderness of the soul, kind of an odyssey of self discovery and renewed purpose."

"I guess I can buy that," I replied, taking another sip of coffee. "But why here, in the Adirondacks?" I asked. "Seems like Alaska would be as good a place as any to conjure up a vision."

LaMont chuckled. "Alaska, the Last Frontier. Where men are men and women win the Iditarod. Yeh, I could have stayed up there, but something was pulling me back to this neck of the woods. There's an energy here, maybe it's my roots, my father and grandfather, hell, maybe you and I had a rendezvous with destiny!" he laughed. "It was just meant to be."

The coffee was tasting even better...LaMont's Otter River Blend and Jack Daniels were a perfect combination.

"I may be ahead of my time," LaMont added.

"What do you mean by that?" I asked.

"Our country has pretty much squandered its wealth. We're drowning in debt. Our government institutions are corrupted and barely function. The economic and environmental apocalypse that's coming may be the perfect storm that sweeps America under the rug of history."

"Pretty goddamn grim there, LaMont," I replied. "This country always comes back. The system is just cleansing itself, that's all."

He threw yet another stone into the river, this time with greater force.

"Spoken like a true Wall Street thug."

"Now we're thugs," I replied, taking another sip of Otter River Jack. "I'm surprised you're so up on current affairs, living as you do."

"I've got a solar charger and wireless router for my laptop," the Last Hermit of the Adirondacks replied with a grin. "But don't tell anyone. You'll ruin my reputation."

We both laughed, and he poured us more bourbon.

151

"Ever read *The Road* by Cormac McCarthy?" he asked. "It's about a father and son wandering through the ashes of a post-apocalyptic America."

"Sounds depressing," I replied.

"You should read it, Flynn. These woods will be teeming with starving refugees—American refugees—in a few years."

He added wood to the fire. The sparks rose into the cold darkness like fireflies dashing away from a burning earth.

"So this vision quest...what have you found out, about yourself?" I asked.

"The most important survival tool is the mind."

"So what's your mind telling you?" I asked.

"I'm still working on it," LaMont replied. "Let's turn in. We'll get an early start in the morning."

I crawled into my sleeping bag and let the anesthesia of fresh-cut balsam carry me instantly to sleep.

Chapter Thirteen

The crackle of a fresh fire and the smell of wood smoke lured me from the soundest sleep I'd had in months. It was still dark but LaMont was already pouring the coffee.

"When you said an early start you weren't kidding," I mumbled, scratching the sleep from my tangled hair. I pulled on my pants and boots, rolled up the sleeping bag, and joined LaMont at the fire. Shards of pink were beginning to break over the eastern sky. He'd set a plate for me of apple slices and buttered bread.

"Eating light this morning," he said, handing me a steaming cup of his Otter Blend, sans the bourbon. "Don't want to weigh you down."

"What's the plan?" I asked, stuffing a chunk of apple into my mouth.

"More of the same," he replied. "I'm not sure what we're looking for, but like I said, we'll know it when we see it."

■　　■　　■

We were back on the river. Ghost-like plumes of icy mist were drifting lazily over the ink-black water. A pair of mergansers, startled by our approach, splashed off a quiet pool, scolding us with a guttural *squawk...squawk.* Their clatter startled a great horned owl, settled in for the day in the thick branches of a white pine. It rose from its perch and flew off into the woods, startling a fishing kingfisher that hastily abandoned its place over the water and darted off ahead of us. Our presence was clearly upsetting the river's natural order of things. We'd paddled quietly for fifteen or twenty minutes, and then the river narrowed like a funnel. I could hear the roar of cascading water ahead of us.

"More rapids?" I shouted.

"The Flume," Lamont yelled back at me. "We'll have to carry around it. Head for that clearing in the birches, just off to the left."

I dug my paddle into the swirling water. The current clearly had the canoe in its grasp.

"A little more muscle up there," LaMont barked, "or we'll be taking the ride of our lives, the last one as well."

Gradually we turned out of the current and paddled into a quiet backwash. LaMont spun the boat around, jumped from the stern seat and yanked the boat onto a narrow slip of sand.

"Grab the waterproof bag and paddles. I'll take the rest," he said, hoisting the canoe onto his shoulders. "Let's go."

The trail rose through a thicket of hemlock. It was well-worn by centuries of river travelers. The roar of the water grew like a high-balling freight train. The footpath was cloaked in a cold mist. It rose like icy smoke from the base of the falls, now more than a hundred feet below us. LaMont stopped and flipped the canoe from his shoulders.

We peered over the edge.

"Phantom Falls," he shouted over the roar of the water.

"I thought you called it The Flume?" I asked.

"There's a legend," he began. "Adirondack Murray wrote about it in his book *Adventures in the Wilderness.* Centuries ago a Huron maiden was swept over the falls. John Plumley, Murray's favorite guide, claimed to have seen her ghost, paddling on the lake just downstream."

We took a long drink of water and pushed on. The trail ran down a steep ridge and soon joined the riverbank. We carried on for a couple of hundred yards, paralleling a series of rock-strewn rapids, which eventually gave way to deeper, smooth-running water. LaMont took the boat from his shoulders and we were under way once again. The river took a sharp turn, and then surprisingly widened into a small lake about half-a-mile wide.

"Pritchard's Lake," LaMont began. "Keep an eye open for that maiden," he added with a laugh. "Back in the early eighteen-hundreds Seth Pritchard damned the river to generate electricity for his hotel and saw mills. The whole shebang burned to the ground in a wildfire in 1908. The ruins might be a nice place to stash some diamonds."

LaMont put down his paddle. A loon, cruising nearby, dove beneath the water.

"Take a break," he said. "Some nice brook trout in here. The water's still a little warm, keeps the trout deep. But let's give it a try."

"Do we have time to fish?"

"There's always time to fish," he replied.

We drifted with a soft wind at our back. LaMont rigged up a fly rod as the sun slipped in and out of the fluffy clouds that coasted over our heads.

"That an eagle up there?" I asked, pointing to a wide pair of wings soaring above the lake just in front of us.

"It's a golden eagle," LaMont replied. "A nesting pair settled in here a couple of years ago, but no chicks yet."

The woods on either shore were thick with sugar maples dressed in varying shades of autumn crimson.

"Pritchard had quite a sugar bush operation back here," LaMont said, handing me the fly rod. He'd tied a grey ghost streamer to a three-foot leader, which was attached to a Lake Clear wabbler like the one Arlo Stoner had rigged up for me.

"I put on a couple of split shot...should take it down twenty feet or so," he added. "Give it a little tweak now and then."

LaMont picked up his paddle and I began letting out line. A loon popped up about thirty yards in front of us. I wondered if it had spotted any trout. I raised the rod tip slightly and settled back. LaMont was paddling us by a water-logged island perhaps an acre in size. It was scattered with small tamaracks and carpeted in leatherleaf.

"That's actually a floating bog," he said. "It moves up and down the lake with the wind."

A pair of mallards that had been resting on one of the bog's shallow pools bolted into the air, quacking angrily as they flew off down the lake.

Something tugged at the line. I struck back.

"Got a hit?" LaMont asked.

The line went slack. "I missed him, or it was weeds."

"You missed him," LaMont said. "The bottom is pretty much rocks."

There was one small island—this one was not a bog—about halfway down the lake. It was marked by a single pine that rose like an arrow into the cobalt-blue sky.

"Osprey nest?" I asked, pointing to mound of large sticks near the top.

"An old one," LaMont replied. "Been empty for years. Too bad."

I didn't get another strike.

"Reel in your line," LaMont said when we'd reached the dam. "We can give it another try when we're back on the river."

He eased the canoe up against two rotted posts.

"We'll get out here."

"Not much of a going concern," I said.

We waded through a meadow of goldenrod and milkweed to the edge of an algae-choked spillway. The remnants of a once hard-working waterwheel hung from a rusted iron axle imbedded into the sides of the stoneworks.

"Pritchard was quite the entrepreneur," LaMont began. "In addition to his hotel, lumber business and the maple syrup, he was bottling pure Adirondack spring water. If he'd charged today's prices, he'd have been a millionaire."

I ran my hand over the massive granite slabs that formed the old spillway and dam. How many men and man-hours must it have taken, without modern equipment, to build such an enterprise in the middle of a wilderness? I wondered.

"Men were men in those days," LaMont said. It was the second time I'd thought he was reading my mind.

We continued across the meadow. The crumbling foundations of several buildings rose through the tangled dogwood and sumac like headstones in a pioneer cemetery. Vesper sparrows and goldfinches darted in and out of dense underbrush.

"There was an ice house…there it is, over there," LaMont said, heading off towards an ivy-covered stone wall. We squeezed through a small stand of aspens and crossed another meadow sprinkled with knee high pine seedlings. The ice house had been dug into a north-facing hillside. The door had long ago fallen from its rusted hinges. We stepped inside just as a horde of squealing bats bolted past our heads on their way out the doorway.

"This must be the place," LaMont said with a soft laugh. He flipped on his flashlight, but not before I stepped face-first into a tangled mass of cobwebs. The dirt floor was carpeted in bat dung, in places several inches thick. A rusted ice saw hung from a hook in one corner, where LaMont was now kneeling.

"Find something?" I asked, still spitting spiders' silk and who knows what else from my mouth.

"I don't know," he replied, pulling a stone block from the wall.

"Na, nothing, just a loose stone."

He slowly played the flashlight around the walls and then on the ceiling.

"I don't know," he said finally, rubbing the toe of his boot through the chalk-colored slime on the floor.

"What?" I asked.

"I wonder if old Louie might have buried it here."

"Under a layer of bat shit?" I asked. "Pretty creative."

"This place burned to the ground just a year or two before my grandfather jumped from that train," LaMont said. He kicked at the floor some more. "Nah, Pritchard may have been still thinking about rebuilding...may have been some people still here. No," he added, heading for the doorway. "This ain't the place."

We spent another hour poking around the ruins, just in case we'd missed something. LaMont told me that Pritchard, having been unsuccessful in finding new investors, had simply vanished into obscurity after the fire had wiped him out.

■　　■　　■

The carry around the dam took us past the spillway and several hundred yards downstream to quiet water. We were under way again, coursing beneath conifers that had miraculously taken root and now prospered atop the boulders that lined both sides of the river.

"Where next?" I asked, watching a single heron lift gracefully from the shoreline and precede us downstream.

"I didn't think we'd find much at Pritchard's," LaMont replied, "but it was worth a look...always enjoy poking around the place. But my grandfather probably high-tailed it past there, just in case anyone was still around. Head for that overhang, now!" he shouted suddenly.

"What is it?" I asked, switching sides with my paddle and digging into the black water.

Womp...womp...womp.

"This guy's getting to be a real pain in the ass," LaMont growled.

We slid under a wind-ravaged hemlock that hung over the water like a feathery umbrella. The chopper roared over us, not five hundred feet from the tree tops.

"It's almost like they're looking for something," I stammered.

"We're not five miles from the compound now. They patrol a pretty wide perimeter."

"What in hell are they hiding?"

"Who knows," LaMont replied.

The helicopter dropped below the tree line.

"Come on, let's go," he said

We continued down river.

■   ■   ■

A series of steep ledges lay directly ahead. As we pulled ashore, a pair of turkey vultures rose awkwardly from the high rocks and drifted off on the rising thermals. Spindly yellow birch trees sprouted from the tops of the larger boulders, their roots running over the rocks like the legs of gigantic spiders. There was no trail to the summit; we rock-hopped our way to the top.

"The drill's the same," LaMont said, heading off in a southerly direction. "We'll meet back here in half an hour or so."

Only lichens, rock mosses, and deer's hair grass could flourish in the cold and wind that relentlessly ripped at the rocks. I watched a dark-eyed junco search for seeds in a bearberry willow. Slim pickings.

Slowly making my way across the north face of the ledge, I found nothing but a handful of shallow, moss-filled crevasses. There were no manageable rocks that could be rearranged. Nothing looked out of place where Louie LaMont might have hidden a cache of stolen diamonds. The junco appeared to be following me, hoping perhaps I'd leave a few crumbs. I apologized for my bad manners.

"See that small lake, off to the north?"

It was LaMont; he'd approached me without a sound.

"Here, take the binoculars," he added.

I scanned the area in which he was pointing. A spec of water rose from the low haze that carpeted the valley below.

"Yeh, I think I can see it. Why?"

"That's the Leache compound."

"I can't see any buildings," I muttered.

"They're there, hidden just behind that rise."

LaMont pulled a plastic bag of jerky from his shirt pocket and handed me a chunk.

"I'm starting to think this is pretty hopeless," I said, snapping off a piece in my teeth. "I mean, look at this," I continued, waving my hand toward the endless mountains that surrounded us.

LaMont smiled and took another chew of jerky.

"I believe if we're to find the diamonds we will find them...there," he said, pointing a long, gnarled finger in a northerly direction.

"The Leache compound?" I stammered. "What in hell are you talking about?"

He rolled up the bag of jerky and put it back in his pocket.

"Let's go."

■　　　■　　　■

Back on the river, LaMont suggested I give the trout another try.

"You're fishing for our dinner, so keep a clear eye," he joked from the back of the canoe.

I flipped the streamer and spoon off the side.

"Let out a little less line," he advised. "Water's shallower here."

The river snaked between banks of silver maple and northern white cedar. The presence of herons and kingfishers boded well for my own angling prospects. LaMont said nothing more about our destination. The only time he spoke was to remind me—more than once—to give my rod tip more action. A small head with two pointed ears was moving silently through the water just off shore.

"Beaver. It won't be there long," LaMont said.

Ka-boom!

The beaver's racquet-like tail hit the water like a bowling ball and it disappeared beneath the surface. We rounded a gentle bend in the river. Four mergansers were heading upstream and closing fast. They zoomed over our heads like fighter jets executing a flyover.

Then I felt something. It wasn't a strike, just a gentle tug on the line. I snapped the rod with my wrist.

"Got him this time?" LaMont asked, the sarcasm dripping from his chapped lips like the sap from the maple trees that graced the shoreline.

I raised the rod tip, palming the reel with my right hand as the fish peeled off eight or ten feet of line.

"Keep him away from the bank," LaMont said, furiously back-paddling the canoe toward the center of the river. "He'll try to snap the leader against that stump."

I raised the rod over my head and was able to retrieve a few feet of line.

"That's it, don't horse him."

I could feel the fish beginning to tire. Gradually I brought him to the boat. LaMont grabbed my fish with his bare hand and flipped it into the canoe.

"Nice brook trout, over two pounds," he said. Its belly was more white than gray. Its speckles of yellow and red sparkled like the jewels we were hoping to find.

"Three more just like that will do just fine," he said, maneuvering the canoe into a deep run along the riverbank.

■　　■　　■

An hour later—our trout dinner secured—we eased the canoe onto a wide sandy beach. There was a lean-to tucked beneath a towering white pine. It was classic Adirondack, crafted of pine logs, facing east where it afforded an unobstructed view of the river and where it would welcome the morning sun.

"We're sleeping in luxury," I offered.

"Yeh, I thought you might like the Marriott, but just for one night," LaMont added. "There aren't many of these old lean-tos left in the Park."

I ducked inside. The logs, smelling of a thousand campfires, bore the carvings of the lean-to's more literate inhabitants:

Magnifique!
But not the black flies!
MF 5/16/05

Joyous Fourth
Feed the mouse, please
Rob and Sue 7/4/89

Elvis Slept Here!

9/8/67

Hayduke Lives!

Another Ed Abbey fan, I thought.

"Remember how to snap off those pine boughs?" LaMont asked.

He didn't wait for my reply.

"You're in charge of our accommodations," he said as he began gathering up firewood. "I'll get dinner started."

■　　■　　■

I followed my nose back to camp, the smell of sizzling bacon and wood smoke pointing the way so clearly I might have made it with my eyes closed. The fish were cleaned and coated with flour. Half a dozen red-skinned potatoes were cooking in a slow boil in an iron pot we'd found hanging in the lean-to. I arranged our beds of boughs and joined LaMont at the fire. He'd already poured me three fingers of bourbon.

"Set a spell," he said, turning the bacon with a forked stick.

The smoke from the campfire rose arrow straight into the early evening sky. Two wood ducks sped by on their way up river.

Whoo—eek...whoo—eek.

And then they were gone.

I took a long sip from my bourbon and decided to ask.

"What exactly did you mean this morning, when you were talking about the diamonds...and pointed off toward Simeon Leache's property?"

LaMont slid the skillet off the fire.

"There was a painting..."

He took a swallow of bourbon and poked at the fire.

163

"A painting...of what?" I asked.

"Funny," he said, still rearranging the fire's coals. "I'd forgotten about it, until this morning." He put down his drink. "There was an old painting...of a waterfall. It hung in our house, in Vermont, over the fireplace. My grandfather had painted it."

"Your grandfather was an artist as well as a guide?" I asked.

"Not really," LaMont replied. "It wasn't a very good painting, but it was a kind of family heirloom, know what I mean? There was a cave behind the falls. You could hardly see it in the painting, but it was there."

He picked up his cup, and after taking a swig of bourbon, returned to messing with the fire's bed of coals.

"I don't get it. What's the painting got to do with Simeon Leache?"

LaMont gave me a wide smile.

"It's elementary, Watson."

I shook my head. "What am I missing here?"

"My grandfather never made it to Vermont, right?" LaMont began. "He lived in this part of the Adirondacks all his life. And he knew this country, every inch of it. So let's suppose, before he jumped from that train, that he knew precisely where he'd hide von Koenig's diamonds, and he made the painting—it looked like it was done in a hurry, or my grandfather thought he was Monet—that he left the painting behind, as a message, in case neither he nor, what was his name...?"

"Aharon Friedman," I replied.

"In case neither one of them made it. Of course no one ever tied my grandfather to von Koenig's missing millions, until now. So no one, my grandmother, my father, hell, even me knew what the painting might be all about."

164

"I'm still not following you," I stammered.

LaMont took a sip of his bourbon. "Fisher Falls."

"Fisher Falls?" I asked.

"It's the only waterfall I know of between here and Lake Champlain."

"You think it was Fisher Falls in the painting...and that there is a cave?"

"I don't have a clue. I've never been there."

"So that's where we're headed tomorrow?" I asked.

"It's not quite that easy," LaMont began. "Fisher Falls is probably half a mile or more inside the Leache compound. He acquired it when he bought the old Twitchell Club property. And Leache has security up the kazoo."

"Wouldn't that be a pisser," I added.

"That Simeon Leache is sitting on the diamonds and doesn't even know it?" LaMont said. "Yeh, I thought of that. But this is a long shot, Flynn. It's still a very long shot."

He slid the skillet back over the coals. The bacon grease began to crackle and pop.

"What ever happened to the painting?" I asked.

"My mother donated it to the library in Ausable. They have some of my grandfather's traps, guns, stuff like that in a little display."

He slid the trout into the skillet.

"Let's eat."

■　　■　　■

If I'd eaten sweeter trout, I couldn't remember when. It was nearly dark when we'd cleaned up the dishes. A coyote across the river welcomed the night with a long wail. LaMont added some thick chunks of yellow birch to the fire. I produced a couple of Pop's Cubans. We lit up and watched our tobacco smoke float into a star-filled, carbon-black sky.

"I didn't realize, until today, how much I've missed this," I said, taking a thoughtful drag on my cigar.

"Missed what?" LaMont asked. His gaze was locked on the flickering flames of the campfire.

"These mountains," I replied. "I had some great times with my own grandfather up here."

LaMont poked at the fire with a stick.

"So what's next for you, Doctor Jones?" he asked.

"Doctor Jones?"

"That fedora you're wearing," he replied, "reminds me of Indiana Jones. You're even a treasure hunter," he added with a soft laugh.

"The hat's my grandfather's. Thought it might bring us some luck," I replied.

"As I was saying, Doctor Jones, are you going back to Greed Street when all this is over?"

"If we find the diamonds I've got to go back. Like you said, we'll be a few million short of what's needed to top Leache's bid. Whatever the diamonds are worth, their value will have to be doubled or tripled."

"So how do you do that? Where do you roll the dice?" LaMont asked. "You could lose the whole shebang."

"The futures market…energy, agricultural products, precious and industrial metals, that sort of thing," I replied. "It can be done. It's all about timing," I added with a wink.

"What if we don't find these diamonds, and that's a very real possibility," LaMont continued. "What then?"

I took another pull on my cigar, blowing the smoke out toward the fire. An owl hooted once, then twice more, letting us know he was keeping an eye on us. "I'm probably done with Wall Street. If by some chance we can save Lost Pond, then, well…"

"You thinking about moving up here?" LaMont asked.

" I don't know…Might be fun to finish my grandfather's book, and there's a woman, back there."

"Ah, there's always a woman," LaMont chortled. "That would be the woman you mentioned? I think her name was Megan?"

"Yeah, that's her, might be worth sticking around." I took another puff on my cigar. "Lost Pond kind of grows on you. It's a collection of certified characters. There's a gourmet French cook who's Turkish, an allegedly gay guide who really isn't gay—he's sleeping with a crippled fly tier's mail order Bosnian bride. There's an alcoholic ex-surgeon from California. That's Doc Ingram. And there's Megan Seagar."

"What's she do in Lost Pond?" LaMont asked.

"Megan's an artist…runs a combination art gallery, book shop, bakery and liquor store."

"The perfect combination," LaMont said. "Does she sell cigars?"

"She does. Megan's a very interesting woman."

LaMont blew a perfect smoke ring into the night sky.

"Well, Flynn, I think you may have it made. All we have to do now is find those diamonds."

167

Chapter Fourteen

The rain began falling just past midnight. It was preceded by a lightning strike that in one fiery instant turned night to day. Thunder rocked the lean-to as if it had been hit by a cannon ball. Then the rains came, sweeping in off the lake, pummeling our camp with hail stones the size of marbles. LaMont was already crawling into his rain gear. I rolled over and looked at my watch. It wasn't quite six.

"Wet son of a bitch," I mumbled.

He handed me a chunk of jerky.

"Breakfast…let's move out," he said, tossing me a pair of rain pants.

Ten minutes later we were back on the river. The rain kept coming, ripping at my face like bits of glass. The good news was that Leache's helicopter was no doubt grounded. I shoved another piece of jerky into my mouth while I longed for a hot cup of LaMont's Otter River coffee. A pair of mergansers paddled past us. Even the ducks weren't flying. The teeming streets of New York seemed a lifetime away. The river had me in its grasp, taking me to a place I did not yet know. LaMont was unusually quiet. We hadn't spoken since breaking camp. I suspected he might be wondering what course his own life might take…if we uncovered von Koenig's diamonds. We both already knew our lives would never be the same.

We paddled on.

■   ■   ■

The conifers were gradually giving way to open

marshland. The river morphed into a sea of grass. We twisted through a floodplain of speckled alders and mountain holly, the rain gradually softening to a misting drizzle. After drifting through groves of willow and dogwood, we paddled out into a small lake. LaMont turned the canoe toward the south shore, embraced with cedars and white birch.

"The mouth of the Fisher River is off to the right."

"How far is it to the falls?" I asked.

"A mile, maybe more" he replied. "Like I said, I've never been here before."

The last storm clouds were drifting off to the southeast. A pair of green-winged teal exploded from the mist, high-tailing it over the marsh. We paddled into the river, but not for long. Our route was blocked by an impenetrable wall of sticks and mud, shoulder high from its base and stretching more than twenty yards across the river. Behind the biggest beaver dam I'd ever seen, the river widened into a pond several acres in size.

LaMont brought the canoe alongside the dam.

"Think you can get out without taking a cold swim?" he joked.

It wasn't easy, but I managed to crawl from the canoe onto the dam without dumping the boat or myself. Several wood ducks blasted off the pond. They took a tight turn, and then flew over our heads back toward the lake.

"This is amazing," I exclaimed. "I'd love to watch them sometime, just to see how they do it."

"They're out here every night, plugging leaks, making it stronger," LaMont said. "It's a matter of life and death for them. If the dam springs a leak this winter, and the water freezes below the entrance to their lodge, they won't be able to reach their food supply. They'll starve to death."

LaMont pulled the canoe over the dam. I managed to

climb back in without incident. Under way again, we crossed the pond and headed upriver. The warm sun was giving way again to thickening storm clouds. In minutes the rain began with a vengeance. The river was rising before my eyes. Digging into the stiffening current, we paddled through stands of tamarack and white pine, then mostly hardwoods, cherry, maple and yellow birch. The channel tightened. The current seemed intent on pushing us all the way back to the Otter River. Fighting the rushing water we maneuvered around three immense dome-shaped boulders. Then the river widened again, but it was mostly rock-strewn, and despite the rainfall, it was too shallow to paddle.

"This as far as we go, by canoe," LaMont said. "Besides, the falls shouldn't be far from here."

We got out and pulled the canoe up on the river bank.

"What now?" I asked.

"We go on foot, Doctor Jones," LaMont replied, "but first we stash the canoe."

He looked around, quickly spotting a tangle of fallen white pines. We tucked the canoe into a snarl of branches, tossing on a couple armloads of sticks for good measure.

"Hope it's here when we get back," LaMont said with a wink.

We picked up a well-worn game trail. It paralleled the river for perhaps half a mile. When it abruptly turned away from the water and deeper into the woods, we stuck to the river's edge, tramping over and crawling under a dozen blowdowns.

Then LaMont stopped. He raised his right hand. I froze.

"What is it, a bear?" I whispered, recalling my previous encounter with Arlo Stoner.

"Not exactly," LaMont replied. "There, on the other side of those birches."

I squinted over his shoulder. "Is that a chain link fence?"

LaMont was already scanning the fence with his binoculars. He handed them to me. "Take a look."

There was a fence all right, and a sign:

WARNING
PRIVATE PROPERTY
PATROLLED AND UNDER ELECTRONIC SURVEILLANCE.
NO TRESPASSING

"Follow me, and keep low," LaMont said. We inched ahead on our hands and knees. The fence was probably ten or twelve feet high. The top was strung with glimmering razor wire. There was a road of sorts on the other side, wide enough for a small Jeep or all-terrain-vehicle.

"I'd heard Leache had fenced off the place, but I didn't believe it," LaMont said.

"What do they mean...*electronic surveillance*?" I asked. "Can they see us...now?"

"Not from here," LaMont replied. "Look, up on that yellow birch. See the solar panel and transmitter? The camera is just underneath. We're out of its sight range."

"How far is to the falls?" I asked.

"Listen," LaMont replied. "You can hear it, though it's probably half a mile upstream."

"And on the other side of the fence," I added. "How do we cross it without being spotted?"

"Very quickly," he replied, pulling what looked like a cell phone from his pocket.

"What are you going to do, call Leache and ask him to open the gate?" I joked.

"I saved a few tools from my past life," he replied. "This will jam the electronics and disable the camera. It'll make it look like some sort of temporary interference."

"But how are we going to get over the fence?" I asked. "That's razor wire."

"We're going to fly." LaMont was grinning from ear to ear. "Adventure, Doctor Jones, adventure!"

We paralleled the fence line for perhaps twenty yards, staying low, making sure to keep out of the camera's sight lines. Then LaMont stopped.

"This is the place."

I didn't have a clue what he meant. The fence looked as imposing as ever. He stripped off his pack and pulled out a rope. There was a small silver grappling hook attached to one end.

"What else have you got in that pack?" I asked.

"You ever a Boy Scout?"

"I know, be prepared," I replied. "But for what?"

LaMont was already climbing a thick-limbed beech tree.

"We've got just a couple of minutes," he said, reaching a long, wide branch about fifteen feet off the ground. He aimed his jamming devise at the camera for about ten seconds. "That should do it," he said. "But we don't have much time."

After looping the rope neatly in his left hand he wound up and flung the grappling hook over the fence.

"Nice shot," I said, watching the hook loop over the sturdy limb of a yellow birch.

He gave the rope a sharp yank, securing the hook's claws into the tree.

"Me Tarzan, you Jane," he laughed.

Then he grabbed the rope and swung over the fence, clearing the razor wire by inches and landing expertly in the crotch of the birch.

I climbed the beech tree. LaMont threw me the rope.

"Go, go, go!" he shouted.

I let fly, but my boot nicked razor wire, throwing me off just enough to miss the landing point. I slammed face first into the trunk of the tree.

LaMont was laughing.

"Well done, Doctor Jones!"

I slid down the rope to the ground. LaMont dislodged the grappling hook, tossed me the rope, and then climbed from the tree.

"You okay?" he asked.

My head hurt like hell, so I lied.

"I think so," I muttered.

"Shit!"

"What?" I asked.

"Your goddamned hat," LaMont snarled.

My grandfather's *lucky* hat was still in the beech tree—on the other side of the fence. I must have caught it in on a branch when I jumped.

"Well, at least it's the right color," LaMont finally said. "Let's hope it stays there. If the wind blows it out of that tree, and they've got dogs, Leache will be on our trail in a heartbeat."

We gathered up our gear. As soon as we'd cleared the sweep of the camera LaMont turned it back on with his jamming device.

"Let's hope they think it was just a blip in their system," he said.

■　　■　　■

We followed the riverbank, continuing upstream, moving deeper onto Simeon Leache's property. I was sure I heard the barking of dogs behind us, but LaMont told me I was imagining things. I was really pissed about losing Pop's hat.

"What if there is no cave? What then?" I asked.

"Then we get the hell out of here before we get shot," LaMont replied.

A cold fog was now drifting through the trees. We rounded a bend in the river and there it was, Fisher Falls. The river tumbled off a ledge of granite more than a hundred feet above us, thundering into a misty, rock-filled canyon the length of a football field. We put our rain gear back on and inched into the knee-deep water. The footing was treacherous on the algae-slick rocks. And we were pushing against a surging, storm-swelled current that could yank our boots from under us at any moment. But we kept moving, clinging to the wet, greasy walls of the canyon, hoping we wouldn't be swept into the rushing water.

Two massive boulders now lay between us and the base of the falls. Wading between them was impossible; the current was too fast. We had to climb up and over. Without the rope and grappling hook we'd never have made it to the base of the falls. If Louie LaMont had come this way nearly a century ago he must have been half salamander, or the river level was much lower. No wonder no one had found the diamonds, if the diamonds were buried somewhere behind the falls at all.

"What now?" I shouted.

We were standing in a shallow pool, out of the current, just off to the side of the thundering cascade.

"There's a ledge behind the falls," LaMont yelled back over the roar of the water. The rock shelf was barely wide enough to walk on, and it was coated with an icy green slime. One slip would be fatal.

"Follow me, and watch your step." LaMont shouted.

He ducked behind the falls and disappeared.

I climbed onto the ledge and began inching my way after him. The howl of the water was deafening. But where was

LaMont? Had he slipped on the algae-covered rocks? Was I on my own, trapped behind tons of falling water?

"Flynn…in here."

He grabbed my arm and pulled me into a narrow crevasse.

"This might be it," he shouted, flipping on his flashlight. "Let's take a look."

I squeezed between the moss-slathered rocks, blindly following the flickering beam of LaMont's light. The roar of the falls was receding behind us. But what if this was a dead end? What then?

"How far do you think this goes?" I finally asked.

"Not far, this is the end of the line. But look at this," he added quickly.

I followed the light toward the ceiling. There was a crack, an opening perhaps wide enough to just squeeze through.

"Think it goes anywhere?" I asked.

LaMont was already pulling himself through.

"Let me take a look," he called back.

And then he was gone, again. Fisher Falls was now just a whisper. I wiped my running nose with the sleeve of my jacket. Despite the rain gear I felt sopping wet.

"LaMont?" I shouted.

Nothing.

"LaMont…are you okay?"

Then I saw a flash from his light on the rocks overhead.

"Holy shit! Wait 'til you see this!" he shouted back.

I pulled myself up through the crevasse. LaMont was playing his light off the walls of an immense cavern. Stalactites hung from the ceiling like mammoth spikes of ivory and ice. The walls were lime green and the air surprisingly warm. He began to peel off his rain gear. I did the same.

"I guess that settles it, about the cave, that is," LaMont

said. "Come on, let's look around."

My heart was pounding like I'd just run a four-minute-mile. Just days ago I'd been drinking a beer in Yankee Stadium. Now I was spelunking through a cave perhaps only a handful of humans had ever seen. The remote chance that we might uncover von Koenig's diamonds suddenly seemed somehow possible. LaMont had already moved toward the center of the cavern, leaving me pretty much in the dark. I stumbled after him.

"Son of a bitch, look at this, Flynn."

LaMont was down on one knee, running his hands through something on the cavern floor.

"It looks like an old campfire," I said. "And look at these!"

"Jesus," LaMont replied, picking up an earth brown clay bowl, one of several scattered about the fire site. "The Mohawks or the Algonquin knew about this place."

He played the light around the floor of the cavernous room.

"Jesus!"

"What is it?" I asked.

"What do you see, Flynn?"

"Those are…footprints, in the sand!" I exclaimed.

"Not just footprints…moccasin prints. Hell, they're probably a couple of centuries old."

"Kinda feel like we've stepped into a museum," I replied.

"Hey, look at this," LaMont added, pointing to another set of tracks. "Boots. You can still see the imprint from the heels. This weren't no Injun."

He was running the tips of his fingers over the boot prints in the soft sand. "Those could be…my grandfather's boots."

We followed the tracks for thirty feet or so, then lost the trail over a wide layer of rock.

"Let's check that opening over there," LaMont said.

He was heading toward what appeared to be the mouth of a tunnel near the back of the cavern.

"Here's another boot print," he said.

But the so-called tunnel was a dead end, just a deep gouge in the rocks.

LaMont moved off in a new direction. I stumbled after him, trailing his wavering light.

"This looks like it might go somewhere," he said.

We squeezed into a wide crack in the cavern wall, finding ourselves in another passageway. The air was a good ten degrees warmer than in the cavern. And there was putrid stench...like the ice house at Pritchard's Lake. Then I heard them coming.

LaMont had already hit the ground.

"Bats!"

I dropped to my knees, wrapping my arms over my head. The air rumbled to the beat of a thousand furious wings. The horde stormed over us, a whirling, wildly shrieking cloud of fur and fangs. And then they were gone.

"To the Batmobile," LaMont laughed as he regained his footing.

We continued on. The passageway twisted and turned, so constricted in places we could barely squeeze through. If this was a dead-end I wondered if we could squeeze our way back out.

Then LaMont stopped. "Here's another boot print. We just might be on the right track."

Fifty feet later the tunnel spilled into another cavern, smaller than the first, about the size of a high school gymnasium. LaMont swept the rock walls with his light. I could feel a cold, damp draft on the back of my neck.

"Another fire pit...even left us some wood."

"How in hell did someone get firewood in here?" I asked.

"There must be another way in here...and out." He stripped off his pack and dropped it by the pit. "Smoke from that fire had to go somewhere. Let's mosey around."

I couldn't be sure, but I had the feeling our only flashlight appeared to be fading.

"How are your batteries?" I asked.

He shined his light near my face.

"Good for a few more hours."

The walls of the cavern were mostly smooth, broken only by occasional cracks no wider than a man's fist. We continued working around the perimeter.

"This looks kind of out of place, wouldn't you say?"

"What?" I asked. "That rock over there?"

LaMont was playing his light on a round stone the size of a beach ball. It had fallen—or had been pushed—against the wall of the cave.

"Hold my flashlight while I see if I can move this thing."

The rock rolled easily away, exposing a crevice in the rocks.

"Too small to crawl through," LaMont said. "Hand me the light."

He wiggled into the rocks, about up to his waist. Then I heard him mumble something.

"What did you say?" I asked

He wormed his way back out.

"I said holy shit!" He reached back into the rocks and handed me a dust-coated canvas bag about the size of a briefcase.

"Hold on to this," he said. "There are three more in there just like it." He squirmed back into the hole.

My hands were shaking and I suddenly needed to pee.

LaMont wiggled back out with three more bags, just like

the first.

"Son of a bitch!" he shouted. "Son...of...a...bitch! Better open one up. Could be full of rocks," LaMont said with a grin.

He held the light. The bags were cinched at the top with leather cords tied off in square knots. My hands still trembling, I managed to untie the first bag.

"I don't think these are rocks," I stammered, pulling out a fistful of diamonds the size of Brazil nuts.

"Like I said...son...of...a...bitch!" he exclaimed. "Well, what now, Doctor Jones?"

■   ■   ■

The light from the campfire skipped over the rock walls like dancers pirouetting across a screen of stone. We'd opted to spend the night in the cave. Finding our way behind the falls and wading the river after dark would be suicide. Dinner consisted of freeze-dried spaghetti and meatballs. I missed the fresh trout already.

"Think who else may have spent a night or two here, besides my grandfather," LaMont said as he poured us both a bourbon. "Algonquin, Mohawk hunters, hell, real cave men," he added.

"Like to come back sometime and really explore this place," I replied. "No telling what you might find."

"As long as it belongs to Simeon Leache, that's going to be a little tricky," the Last Hermit of the Adirondacks replied. "But count me in," he quickly added.

I needed to take a whiz. Wandering over to a corner of the cave to relieve myself, something caught my eye. It was lying near the wall just out of the light.

"Bring the flashlight over here."

"Can't find your Johnson?" LaMont joked.

"Very funny. No, what's that, over there by the wall?"

LaMont played the light along the floor of the cave.

"That, my friend, is the rib cage of a deer."

"How would a deer get down here?" I asked.

"Dead," LaMont replied. " Coyote, wolf, maybe a cougar dragged it in."

"There aren't any wolves or mountain lions in the Adirondacks, are there?"

"They're here. Believe me, they're here."

Chapter Fifteen

The wolf was ripping at my sleeping bag. I could feel its steaming, odorous breath in my face.

But it was LaMont.

"Get up. We've got to get moving…now."

I think I'd slept with one eye open, half expecting a snarling pack of wolves was about to tear me to shreds.

"We've got company," he added.

I pulled off the sleeping bag and staggered to my feet.

"Company? What in hell are you talking about?"

"Listen," he replied.

Then I heard it, too, the faint baying of dogs.

"Leache's patrols must have found your goddamned hat, Doctor Jones. Or we missed a surveillance camera. They're hot on our trail now."

"How are we going to get out of here?" I asked.

"Been thinking the same thing," LaMont replied with a smile. "The smoke from our fire? It's been curling up through that crevasse, there."

He played his flashlight, its beam now weakening by the minute, on a banana-shaped opening we'd missed in our search of the cave. It looked just wide enough to squeeze through.

"Whatever dragged that deer in here…that has to be the way out."

He grabbed our gear. I took the diamonds. We made for the crevasse.

The dogs were gaining ground as we wiggled into the rocks. Luckily, the passage widened and we could break into a

181

slow run. We'd covered perhaps fifty yards when LaMont suddenly stopped.

"What is it?" I asked, welcoming a chance to catch my breath.

"Looks like we're going to drop into another cave," he replied. "It's only about three feet down, but watch your step. Don't break an ankle."

LaMont jumped. I followed.

A primordial cry, wild and furious, drove LaMont back into me as if he'd been hit with a thunderbolt.

"Over there," he gasped, waving his light just in front of us.

"Jesus! It's a mountain lion!" I stammered.

The cat's emerald eyes simmered in the dimming beam of LaMont's flashlight.

"Don't friggin' move," he whispered.

"Move? I'm pissing my pants," I whispered back.

The mountain lion was crouched on its front legs, its shoulder muscles rippling like coiled springs. It could be on us in a single bound. But the big cat suddenly turned and in one graceful move jumped to a narrow ledge some six feet away. It looked back at us for a second or two and then disappeared into the rocks.

"Holy shit!" I finally gasped.

"Remember to thank that cat when this is over," LaMont said. "It just showed us the way out of here."

We climbed onto the ledge. The cougar had vanished through a passageway that was just wide enough for us to crawl through. The tunnel twisted and turned over shards of jagged rocks that ripped at our hands and knees. We could still hear the dogs. And they were closing. Then I smelled fresh air. Shafts of sunlight were glimmering off the rock walls just in front of us.

And then we were out, standing on a wide shelf of sparkling granite speckled with white paper birch trees. The mouth of the tunnel was well hidden behind several massive boulders.

"No wonder no one's found this place," LaMont said, reaching for his water bottle. "Make a nice camp, once Leache is out of the way."

I wondered what *out of the way* meant, but I didn't ask. After twelve wet, mostly cold hours underground I was content to let the warm morning sun pour over me like a hot shower.

LaMont was looking around, searching for his bearings.

"Where are we?" I asked.

"I'll be damned," he replied. "We're off the compound. We're on the north side of Sentinel Peak."

"What about the dogs...and the canoe? How do we get back to the river?" I asked.

"We're not going back to the river," LaMont replied. "We'll bushwhack our way to the tracks...a couple of miles from here."

"But what about the dogs?" I asked again.

"When Leache's hounds pick up the cat's scent, they'll be off and running, and not after us. Remember that cougar in your prayers. It saved your ass."

■　　■　　■

LaMont was right; the dogs headed off to the west. We never heard them again.

"Why the rail line?" I gasped. Keeping up with LaMont was like running a marathon. We'd come down from Sentinel Peak and were wading yet another icy stream. "You have another one of those little rail cars stashed somewhere?"

"You're learning," LaMont laughed.

"What about the canoe?" I asked.

"I'll leave it there 'til this is over," he replied. "Not my only canoe, you know."

It was now clear how LaMont was able to move quickly from one place to another, avoiding detection with ease.

Stopping just once for some jerky and a long drink of water, we worked our way around two wide marshes, reaching the rail line shortly after noon. LaMont looked up and down the tracks.

"Didn't come out exactly where I'd planned," he said. "We're about a quarter mile off...this way."

We started walking. The sun told me we were headed south.

The rail corridor was thick with aspen trees. Their leaves rattled like chimes in the soft October breeze. Chunks of twisted steel littered both sides of the tracks, the rusting remains of a derailment or a fatal head-on collision, grim calamities that marked the railroad's storied history. Black-capped chickadees darted in and out of the sumac that prospered on the edges of the oil-soaked gravel track bed.

LaMont's rail car was hidden in a bramble of dogwood and sumac. It was built much like the one we'd used before, basically a platform powered with a small gasoline motor. We carried it to the tracks. I climbed on with the diamonds. LaMont yanked the starter cord once, then twice. The engine sprang to life. The Hermit kept his equipment in good running order.

We started down the tracks, gradually reaching our top speed of about twenty-five miles per hour. I took a long drink, emptying my last water bottle. For the first time in four days I felt just a hint of control coming back into my life.

"Those guys, with the dogs...do you think they have any

idea who we were or what we were after?" I asked.

"Good question," LaMont replied. "Simeon Leache may be an idiot, but he's no fool."

"Think he's heard anything about von Koenig...the legend...the missing millions?" I asked.

"Probably," LaMont replied. "Rumors have been flying for years, even about diamonds. But no one ever proved it, until your grandfather. Will Leache put it all together? I don't know. That hat you lost, Doctor Jones. Can he trace it back to you?"

"There's a pin..."

"What kind of pin?"

"A Lost Pond pin. They sell them in the Friends' gift shop. And my grandfather's initials—RGF—are written inside, on the band."

"I wouldn't stick around Lost Pond if I were you," LaMont replied.

The terrain began to look familiar. We sped past the trailhead we'd taken coming off the Hogback. I guessed Lost Pond wasn't more than half an hour away.

"So what's next?" I asked. "You heading back to the hermit's life?"

"It's a damn fine life, Flynn," LaMont replied. "I know you'll forget everything you've seen, the cave on the Hogback, my transportation system. Otherwise I'll have to terminate you...with extreme prejudice."

I swallowed hard. "What cave? I've never seen you in my life."

LaMont was laughing. "Do you really think you can pull it off, this financial high wire act...leveraging the diamonds, saving Lost Pond from Simeon Leache?"

"It's a long shot," I admitted. "The stars are going to have to align perfectly. Time isn't on our side."

"My mission's complete," LaMont said. "Just don't screw the pooch."

"Screw the pooch?" I asked.

"Navy term…Don't fuck up. Kind of ironic, isn't it?" LaMont added.

"What's that?"

"Von Koenig's fortune, once headed to Nazi Germany, may help put an end to Simeon Leache. The guy's got a lot in common with Adolph Hitler, don't you think?"

"I never thought of it that way," I replied, "but you're right."

He began easing up on the throttle.

"Lost Pond's just around the bend, about a quarter mile," he said, gradually bringing the flatbed to a stop. "This is as far as I go. Give me a hand turning this bugger around."

We jumped off and quickly had the car headed back up the line.

"How do I thank you?" I began. "There are some fine people in Lost Pond who will owe you more than they'll ever know."

"When you stick it to Leache, give it a twist for me."

We shook hands.

"Good luck, Doctor Jones."

Ethan LaMont opened the throttle, and the Last Hermit of the Adirondacks disappeared around the bend in the tracks.

Chapter Sixteen

I didn't want to be seen with the diamonds, so I cut through the woods to Pop's cabin. It was just past five. I stuffed the four canvas bags in the wood box on the deck and headed for *La Mouche Noire*. I hoped Doc Ingram would be holding down the bar. He didn't disappoint.

"You're back," he said, saluting me with his near empty martini glass.

"I could use a drink," I replied.

"And I could use another. The bar is open!" Doc crowed.

Sandy was, as usual, nowhere in sight.

Doc stepped behind the bar. "The first one's on me. By the way, you look like a piece of shit."

I stared into a mirror advertising *la Divine St. Landelin*. I guessed it was some kind of French beer. Doc was right. The skin on my face was raw from the wind and sun, cracked and umber brown, like a slab of bacon left too long in a sizzling skillet. My eyes sagged from their sockets like rotting plums. I'd raised a beard, six days' worth. The predominance of gray in my steely stubble was an unwelcome surprise. Doc slid my martini down the bar. I took the glass in my scab-covered hand and took a long, deep, slow sip.

I felt better already.

"Well?" Doc asked. "Was it a wild goose chase...or not?"

"Or not," I replied, toasting him with my glass. I took another long drink.

Doc's eyes widened. He scanned the empty dining room again, as if someone might be listening, hiding under a table or behind a curtain.

"Diamonds?" he whispered. "You found the fuckin' diamonds?"

"We've got to move fast," I replied. "I'll fill you in later."

"Did you find that hermit guy?" he asked, downing his martini in two rushed swallows. "Stoner said he put you on his trail."

"I did. I'd never have found the diamonds without him."

"Son of a bitch," Doc muttered, biting into the last of his martini's jalapeno-stuffed olives.

"Where's Megan?" I asked.

"She was in Syracuse, but got back yesterday," he said. "She's probably at her shop."

I walked behind the bar, pouring the remains of my martini into a plastic beer cup.

"A roadie," I said. "I'll get Megan. Meet me at my grandfather's place. And Doc, if you see anyone, anything that looks out of place...come back here."

"What's the matter?"

"Later," I replied, rushing for the door.

■　　■　　■

"You're back!" Megan shouted, giving me a warm hug. She lingered in my arms just long enough to let me know she meant it. I'd found her on the shop's porch where she was setting some of her paintings on easels.

"Hakeem's got a boatload of leaf peepers coming out for dinner. Might sell a painting tonight, never know," she said, giving me another hug.

"Close up, now," I said. "I need your help."

■　　■　　■

I filled Megan in on our way to Pop's cabin. Reaching the

top of the driveway a loon's wild wail rolled across the lake. Megan stopped. The loon cried again.

"I never get tired of that," she said, dropping her head on my shoulder. I kissed her softly on the forehead. We stared out through the bare trees to the lake.

"Did you hear that?" I asked.

"What?"

"Sounds like a helicopter," I replied.

We listened for a moment, but all we heard was the wind.

The lights were on in the kitchen. We could smell the wood smoke curling up from Pop's chimney into a twilight-streaked sky. Doc had already started a fire.

"Are the diamonds here, in the cabin?" Megan asked.

I opened the kitchen door.

"They're here, four bags full," I replied.

Doc was making a martini as we walked in.

"Freshen that up?" he asked, taking the plastic cup from my hand.

Megan headed for the refrigerator for a beer.

Drinks in hand, we settled in Pop's living room. The fire was already working its magic.

"I've got to get to my car tonight," I began.

"Arlo could take you," Doc said, looking at his watch. "He's bringing a boatload of tourists out from the Landing...should be here any minute."

"Why tonight?" Megan asked. "What's the matter, Ryan?"

"There's a chance that Leache could trace the diamonds back here," I replied. "I'll skip the details, but the sooner I can get back to the city the better."

"What do you need us to do?" she replied.

"It will take me twenty minutes or so to get my stuff together," I said. "Doc, meet Arlo when he ties up, tell him to gas up the fastest boat he's got. Megan, you've got to reach Winnie Stephenson. Tell her another party is preparing to top Leache's offer, one she and the college will be very happy with—but she's got to keep it quiet, and keep her distance from Leache and his attorneys."

"What are you going to do?" Megan asked.

"The first thing is sell the diamonds. I think I know someone who can help me, and be very quiet in the process. Then, well, we'll see what the futures market has to offer. It's complicated...it might not work, but it's our only chance. I don't have to tell you how sensitive, how dangerous this is. No one but the three of us has to know what we've done or what we are going to try to do...to save Lost Pond."

Doc Ingram raised his glass. "I'll drink to that."

"Go right ahead. It might be your last."

Simeon Leache was lumbering across the room toward us. He was flanked by two thickset, hulking men. One was olive-skinned, with jet-black hair combed into a pony tail. There was a jagged scar running from beneath his right ear across his cheek to the edge of his lip. The other man had yellowish blonde hair that touched his shoulders. His eyes were the color of blue ice. Both were dressed in black turtleneck sweaters and black denim trousers. Both were wearing side arms.

"You forgot your hat, Mr. Flynn," Leache said, tossing me Pop's fedora. It sailed across the room like a Frisbee, landing square in my lap.

"I don't know what you're talking about," I countered. "Who do you think you are, just bursting in here?"

The blonde-haired man was moving toward Megan and Doc.

"Don't jerk me around, Flynn," Leache snarled. "Where are they?"

"I don't know what you're talking about," I replied,

getting up from my chair.

The scar-faced man grabbed me by the throat and lifted me off the floor with a single hand. Smiling while I twisted in the air, he threw me back into the chair.

"You also forgot one of these," Leache said. He opened his hand. He was holding one of the diamonds. It must have slipped from my hands back in the cave. Doc's and Megan's eyes widened. Even the goons were transfixed by the stone's seductive charm.

"You found von Koenig's lost fortune," Leache continued. "You found it on my property. That, my friend, makes the diamonds MY property. I want them back. I want them back now!"

"Von who?" I stammered, gasping for breath.

Simeon Leache nodded to the blond-haired man, who pulled a black-handled knife from a sheath strapped to his leg. Its serrated blade glistened in the flickering light of the fire. Grabbing a handful of Megan's hair, he yanked her head back and stuck the point of the knife just deep enough into Megan's neck to draw blood.

Doc charged across the room. "Get your goddamned hands off her!"

The scar-faced man buried one of his massive fists into Doc's stomach, the other he drove squarely against Doc's jaw. Rocked off his feet, Doc fell backwards, slamming his head into the granite mantle of the fireplace. He was unconscious, perhaps already dead, before his limp body hit the floor.

"Don't push me any further, Flynn," Leache shouted, his face now the color of a ripe beet. Rivulets of sweat were rolling down his forehead, across his sagging jowls and onto the front of his wet wrinkled shirt.

"Hand over the diamonds and no one else will get hurt," he added, glaring at Megan. The blond-haired man shoved the tip of the knife deeper into her neck. She was sobbing now, unable to hold back her tears.

"One last time…where are the diamonds?"

"I came up here to settle my grandfather's estate. That's all."

"You're a liar, and a very bad one," Leache replied. He pulled a photo from his pocket. There we were, LaMont and me, wading toward the falls. We'd missed a surveillance camera. LaMont's face was obscured. He couldn't be identified. But my face was perfectly in focus, unquestionably clear.

"I don't know who was with you, but that, Mr. Flynn, is you. We discovered the cave entrance, behind the falls, two years ago. It's going to be…well, that's none of your business."

He walked behind Megan and ran his thick, sausage-like fingers through her hair and then over her tear-streaked cheeks.

"Such a pretty woman…Yuri has a way of making people talk. Need I say more?"

I looked at Doc, sprawled on the floor. One life may have already been lost. And for what now was clearly a lost cause. No one else was going to die. I had to admit we'd found the diamonds, but…maybe there was still a way out. I decided to take one last chance, to buy us more time, for what I didn't know.

"Leave her alone. She had nothing to do with this. I'll tell you everything," I stammered.

Leache nodded. The man he'd called Yuri removed his knife from Megan's bleeding neck.

"Talk, Flynn. Your time is running out," Leache said.

"Sorting through my grandfather's affairs I discovered he'd been researching the von Koenig legend, the lost fortune," I began.

Leache removed his hat, wiping his sweating brow with his handkerchief.

"Go on, Mister Flynn, please go on."

"I had a few days, so, what the hell, I hired a guide and we set off on a treasure hunt. I had no illusions that we'd find anything. I did it as a last gesture for my grandfather, who believed he'd solved the mystery. It was great fun. Then we found the diamonds. I didn't want to bring them back here. So Wayne, my guide, took them with him to Lake Placid. I'm going to meet him there tomorrow."

Leache looked at Yuri who shook his head just slightly.

"You're lying," Leache said matter-of-factly. "I don't approve of Yuri's methods. But you leave me no choice." He nodded to both men. Yuri grabbed Megan's left wrist, twisting just enough to make her cry out. Then he jammed her hand onto the surface of the table. I lunged toward her, but the scar-faced man tripped me with the tip of his boot. I hit the floor face first. He was on me in an instant, driving his knee into the small my back. I looked up just as Yuri was bringing the jagged blade of his knife down on Megan's fingers.

"I understand that you are an artist," Leache said. "What a waste."

Yuri bore down on his knife.

Megan screamed.

"Stop it!" I cried. "That's enough!"

Leache nodded, waving Yuri off. Blood was oozing from Megan's fingers, but they were still attached.

I looked up at Leache. "The diamonds are in the woodbox, out on the deck,"

"Kiril," Leache barked. The scar-faced man left me on the floor and headed for the deck. Yuri pulled out his pistol, cocked it, and put the barrel to the back of Megan's head.

Leache stared down at me. "If you're stalling, Flynn..."

The scar-faced Kiril returned with the diamonds. Leache opened each bag, his eyes bulging as he ran his hands through the glittering stones.

"Thank you, Flynn," Leache said finally. "Thank you for your generous contribution to my institute."

Doc began to moan. He rolled over on his back. Thank God he was alive.

"I suggest you attend to your friend," Leache said.

I crawled to Doc's side, lifting his head in my arms.

"Do not follow us, or your lady friend will lose more than a few fingers," Leache added.

Yuri took a black hood from his pocket and pulled it over Megan's head. Grabbing her under the arms, he dragged her from the room.

"You won't get away with this," I shouted.

Leache laughed, tipping the brim of his Stetson.

"Who would believe you, Flynn?" he replied.

And then they were gone.

Doc opened his eyes.

"What happened?" he groaned.

I took my handkerchief and wiped at the blood running from the corner of his mouth.

"It's over, Doc," I whispered. "It's over."

Chapter Seventeen

The woodpecker was back, pounding the dead birch next to Pop's cabin with ferocious urgency. Perhaps it sensed an early winter. It was just past seven. I was sprawled on the couch in the den, watching the morning sun creep toward me across the pine-planked floor. I'd crashed there after it was all over. But for most of the night sleeping was a lost cause. Megan was in the bedroom. I hoped she was still asleep. Surprisingly, she'd been released, just before Leache and his helicopter had lifted off. There'd been some shouting, she'd said, between Leache and someone. It was a voice she hadn't heard before. She guessed it was the pilot. She'd been warned not to remove her hood. So she didn't see anyone or hear what they were saying. We'd patched Doc up, with his help, of course. He insisted he was okay so we'd taken him back to his place. There was no way Megan could spend the night alone. Not after what she'd been through. I rolled off the couch and headed for the kitchen and started hustling up some breakfast.

■　　■　　■

"Good morning." Megan was standing in the doorway, wrapped in one of Pop's Hudson Bay blankets. "That bacon smells pretty good. Got any coffee?"

I put down my fork and gave her a long hug. "I didn't want to wake you. How are you feeling...okay?" I said, holding her bandaged hand in mine.

"Yeah, I guess," she said, kissing me lightly on my chapped lips.

"We're damn lucky. It could have been a lot worse," I

said.

"No one would believe us, would they?" she asked.

"Maybe, but probably not," I replied. "Besides, it would only make things worse, for the Friends, the college, everyone. It's over. Simeon Leache won. We lost."

"It's not your fault…you did everything you could. I think your grandfather is very proud of you." She kissed me again, this time parting her lips just slightly. "Where's that coffee? "

I poured her a steaming mug and refilled my own. While I finished up the bacon and scrambled some eggs, Megan took a hot shower and got dressed.

"I feel better already," she said, digging into her eggs. "We should have called Doc."

"Let him sleep," I replied. "I'll buy him a martini before I leave this afternoon."

"So soon?" she replied, reaching for my hand.

"I have a friend, an attorney in New York. He may be able to throw enough roadblocks in Leache's way to slow him up a little…and we can hope for a miracle. I feel so badly for you, the Friends, this nutty place called Lost Pond. I was thinking about moving up here, starting a new life…if things had worked out differently."

I was hoping a possible legal challenge might mean I could put off clearing out Pop's cabin. I didn't want to give the place up. And I didn't want to give up Megan Seagar. "Last night…you said you heard shouting…just before the helicopter took off?" I asked. "Did you hear anything of what was said?"

"There was so much noise. And I had that hood over my head," Megan began. "I thought I heard Leache yell something…like…*who the hell are you?* I just don't know."

I reached across the table and ran my hand through her still damp hair. "I'm sorry. We almost pulled it off."

196

She smiled. "We knew the end was coming, Winnie Stephenson as much as said so at the Friends' spring meeting. We've been hoping an angel would drop out of the sky."

"I'm sorry I wasn't that angel," I replied.

"You are," she replied, squeezing my hand. "When are you leaving?"

"I asked Arlo to stop by around noon."

She glanced at the old Genny Beer clock over Pop's stove.

"It's only eight-thirty."

■　　■　　■

The Major, sputtering and coughing, let us know Arlo Stoner was coming long before he stepped through the kitchen door. He'd kept the dilapidated truck running, just in case this might be its last trip.

"Sorry to disturb you," he said with a mischievous, *I know what you've been up to* grin. "Wind's coming up…like to get you to the Landing and be back before she tears loose. There's a cold front heading in from Canada."

"I'll toss my gear in the truck and meet you at the dock," I said. "Megan and I will walk down."

Stoner smiled again.

"We'd like to stop by Doc's…to say goodbye." We wanted to check on him, to make sure he was okay. But of course Arlo Stoner knew nothing of what Doc, Megan and I had been through the night before.

■　　■　　■

Doc was on his porch, tending to his surprisingly still thriving marigolds. "Trying to stretch these as long as I can," he said. "I've been covering 'em up every night for three

197

weeks." He emptied his watering can on the last pot. "Lucky they're still here...lucky we're all still here," he added. "Have a seat."

We sank into three stick wood rocking chairs.

"How are you feeling, Doc?" Megan asked.

"Ribs are a little tender, couple of loose teeth, and a nice bump on the back of my head. But I'll live."

Then he smiled, giving Megan a sly wink.

"You don't look the worse for wear, young lady."

Doc didn't miss a thing.

"And I suppose you're heading back to the big city," he added.

I explained my Hail Mary legal strategy.

"Nothing is permanent, son. Look what I've been through the last few years, hell, what I've been through in the last day," Doc added. "I will miss our martinis, though."

"We're not through drinking yet," I said. "I'll be back. Hold down the bar."

We shook hands. Megan gave Doc a warm hug. "I'll have a martini with you tonight," she added.

"The bar opens at five!" Doc shouted as we walked back toward the road.

■　　■　　■

Stoner fired the outboard. A thick plume of blue, oil-sopped smoke curled out over the water. I climbed into the boat, waved goodbye to Megan, and said goodbye to Lost Pond, at least for a few weeks.

The air was clear and cold, like one of Doc's martinis. The water in the bay was just a ripple, but I could see white caps already rolling out in the lake. I asked Stoner to stop for a minute at the beaver lodge. I wanted to say goodbye to Pop.

"Rufus was one hell of a man," Stoner said, easing the boat alongside Pop's resting place. I reached out and grabbed hold of the satellite dish. I hoped I wasn't interfering with his reception. Stoner throttled down to a bare idle.

Pop, we almost did it, you and me, and Ethan LaMont. I'm sorry things didn't work out the way you'd hoped. And I'm sorry I didn't get up here to see you, like I'd promised. Who knows how things might have worked out. God speed, Pop. And God bless the New York Yankees."

I pushed us off. We headed out into the lake. Then Stoner tapped me on the shoulder.

I turned around.

"One for Rufus," he shouted, taking a long drink of bourbon. He handed me the bottle.

I took a sip, then another, and watched the shoreline slide away from us.

■　　■　　■

The Landing was just coming into sight when a helicopter howled past us, not two hundred feet above the water.

It wasn't Simeon Leache.

"U.S. Army, Fort Drum," Stoner shouted over the growl of the motor. "Ranger calls them for search operations. They love the practice."

"Something's going on," I shouted back.

Stoner was already looking through his binoculars.

"More boats up ahead...and another chopper, state police."

He handed me the glasses. The Landing was jammed with fire trucks, ambulances, sheriff and state police cars, and other emergency vehicles.

"Never seen this much equipment," Stoner said.

199

A Boston Whaler, clearly marked *New York State Police*, pulled alongside.

"This is a restricted area," a slicker-clad trooper barked.

The water was thick with oil and chunks of smoldering flotsam. My first thought was a plane crash.

Stoner made a wide swing and brought the boat to a dock a hundred yards or so below the Landing. I grabbed my gear.

"There's Cheyenne," Stoner said. "Let's see what she knows."

Cheyenne Levine was standing on shore, serving coffee to half a dozen helmeted firemen.

"What the hell's going on?" Stoner asked

"Simeon Leache. He's dead," she replied. "They just brought in his body, or what was left of it."

"Leache?" I stammered, swallowing hard to keep my breakfast in my stomach.

"I was closing the bar about eleven last night," she continued. "There was a flash, out on the lake, lit up the whole damn sky. Then there was an explosion, shook a couple of bottles right off the back bar. They say it was Leache's helicopter. Nothing official yet, of course, but it was him."

"Was…there anyone with him?" I asked. What I really wanted to know was whether anything else was found, like four canvas bags filled with diamonds.

"They've recovered three other bodies, body parts, that is," she replied.

I could have told her there were two security guards, the pilot and Leache, but of course, how would I know?

"That helicopter blew to bits," Levine continued. "They won't find anything bigger than a beer tray. Wonder what Leache was doing over here that time of night?" she added almost as an afterthought.

Well, Pop, Simeon Leache didn't have the diamonds very

long. They're lost forever now.

Four men were dead. But how could I feel sorry of them? They might have killed Doc, Megan, too, maybe all three of us.

"I need a drink," Stoner said, heading for the Tumble Inn. "How 'bout a roadie?"

"I'll take a rain check," I replied. "I've got a long drive ahead of me. Thanks, Stoner," I added, shaking his hand. "Thanks for everything."

"Watch your intersections, and may all your lights be green, sport," Stoner said. He tipped his cap and waded into the crowd.

Half a dozen volunteer firemen, their meaty hands wrapped around white foam cups of steaming coffee, eyed me suspiciously as I walked across the parking lot and unlocked the Corvette. I threw my gear on the passenger seat, climbed in, and turned the key. The rumble of the engine told me I was leaving one world, heading back to another. I let the oil warm a little. The scene in my windshield was like watching a disaster movie on widescreen: helicopters crisscrossed the sky; crews of frantic technicians were setting up satellite feeds, red lights were flashing everywhere. I scrunched down in the seat. I felt like I was going to puke.

There was a knock on the window. I rolled it open a crack.

"Hey, buddy, ya gotta move it."

I closed the window, shifted into first and eased out of the parking lot. Emergency equipment was still streaming up the road. Every volunteer fire department within a hundred miles probably wanted in on the action, to say they worked the Simeon Leache crash. Maybe their neighbors would see them on CNN.

I was about a mile from the Landing when I noticed a

folded slip of paper tucked in the corner the Corvette's passenger-side visor. It hadn't been there before. I was sure of it. I took it down and flipped it open in my right hand.

Don't screw the pooch.

Holy shit!

I slammed on the brakes. The Corvette slid over the loose gravel, stopping finally at the edge of a gaping ditch. I turned around and looked behind the seats.

There were four canvas bags.

They were still wet.

LaMont! You son of bitch!

EPILOGUE

LOST POND. ONE YEAR LATER.

The American flag fluttered gently on a soft and surprisingly warm October breeze. The dedication ceremony was nearly complete. The new Lost Pond Center for the Creative Arts was open for business. I was seated on the dais with Oliver Scott, who was representing the Friends of George I. Gurdjieff. An audience of perhaps a hundred dignitaries—state officials, cultural leaders, members of the Friends and their families—were seated in the just-completed sculpture garden overlooking Lake Mohawk. Winnie Stephenson was concluding the official transfer of Lost Pond from William and Marshall College to the North Country Creative Coalition—the NCCC—the newly created nonprofit foundation that would now own and operate the historic Adirondack community.

"William and Marshall College and the Friends of George I. Gurdjieff wish to express their deep-felt appreciation to the anonymous donor whose gift of eight million dollars served as the cornerstone for funding the purchase of Lost Pond, thus ensuring its historic and creative legacy," Stephenson told the audience.

Megan and Doc were seated in the front row. We shared a smile. We alone knew how the eight million dollars was raised. In a series of private transactions, I was able to convert von Koenig's diamonds to $2.7 million in cash. Then I caught a break. The Federal Reserve would roil financial markets with a devastating forecast for the U.S. economy. But thanks to a connected friend, I knew several days in advance what the Fed's chairman would reveal in his congressional testimony. Call it insider information, unethical, probably illegal. But the good that would result from my actions was worth bending the rules...just once. I knew after the Fed's forecast was made public, the U.S. dollar would sink to record lows. Energy and agricultural prices would surge. Simply put, I bought low and sold high. A consortium of nonprofit land trusts raised an additional $2 million, which made the Lost Pond purchase possible. Ethan LaMont, whose role in saving the historic landmark would forever remain unknown, had vanished. There'd been no evidence of his breaking into any camps the past winter. Authorities said that his trail had gone ice-cold.

"It is with great pleasure," Stephenson continued, "that I introduce the new executive director of the Lost Pond Center for the Creative Arts. He brings a ferocious commitment to the preservation of the Adirondacks and the financial skills to ensure that the artistic and creative mission of the Center prospers for generations to come. Please welcome Ryan Flynn."

I'd volunteered for the job. My salary requirements were zero. How could the Center's board say no? Funding the property purchase was just the beginning. New revenue streams would be needed. A long-term endowment had to be established. And I was eager to start a new life, one of good works. My remarks were brief, expressing my thankfulness for the preservation of Lost Pond and charting the Center's course for the year ahead. Wrapping up my address I couldn't help notice a late comer to the proceedings. Or perhaps he'd been there all along. He wasn't sitting with the others, but was standing in the shadows at the edge of the woods. What caught my eye were his clothes. He was wearing a nut-brown tweed jacket and tan slacks. I had a similar jacket and slacks hanging in Pop's closet. I couldn't make out the man's face. He was wearing dark sunglasses and a Scottish style touring cap. I had a hat just like it, too. Catching my eye, he gave me a casual salute. I turned away for a moment, acknowledging the enthusiastic applause of the audience. But something drew my eyes back to the woods.

The man was gone.

The ceremony over, the shaking of hands began, followed by a wine and cheese reception. When the last dignitaries had departed, Megan and I decided on a celebratory martini. Of course we invited Doc. We walked back to Pop's cabin, now our home. Megan and I had added a master bedroom with its own fireplace, enlarged the kitchen, and put on a new roof. With the Lost Pond deal complete, we could begin making our wedding plans.

"It's a shame Ethan LaMont wasn't here today," Megan said. "If it hadn't been for him this place would be plowed under by now." She squeezed my hand and smiled. "And WE wouldn't be happening."

"I was coming back for you one way or the other," I replied, kissing her softly on the cheek.

"Arlo told me this morning the FAA's report on the Leache crash is finally official," Doc said. "They've determined it was a ruptured fuel line that caused the helicopter to explode over the lake. Case closed."

"And no one will ever connect Ethan LaMont to the death of Simeon Leache," Megan added.

"I should have guessed LaMont would follow me back here that day," I said. "He knew Leache would come for me."

It hadn't taken us long to figure it out. LaMont must have disabled the pilot and was waiting for Leache and his thugs when they returned to his helicopter with the diamonds. That was what the shouting was about, what Megan couldn't hear over the roar of the motor. LaMont had to have flown the helicopter from Lost Pond to the Landing, dropping the diamonds in the shallows near the beach. Then he flew back out over the water, set some sort of detonation devise, and jumped from the helicopter before it exploded. After swimming to shore he stashed the diamonds in my car and disappeared back into the mountains. He certainly had the training and experience to pull off such a daring and heroic act.

It was a secret we'd share for the rest of our lives.

We'd reached the cabin.

"The bar is open," Doc announced.

Megan gave me a quick kiss. "I'll help Doc get the drinks."

I walked into the den to start a fire. My tan slacks, tweed jacket and cap were laid neatly across the back of Pop's chair. There was a note tucked in the jacket's breast pocket.

Well done, Doctor Jones.

CPSIA information can be obtained at www.ICGtesting.com
Printed in the USA
BVOW040637121011

273424BV00001B/5/P